ROCKSTAR HEARTS

CASH ME OUTSIDE DUET

EDEN FINLEY

LOCKED HEART
&
THORNED HEART

By Eden Finley
Copyright © 2020 by Eden Finley

Professional beta read by Les Court Services.
https://www.lescourtauthorservices.com

Proofread by One Love Editing
http://oneloveediting.com/

❀ Created with Vellum

LOCKED HEART

PROLOGUE

CASHTON

OUR SWEATY BODIES COLLIDE, our breaths mingle, and even though I can feel his skin on mine, his heartbeat under my hand, I know this is goodbye.

I'm pinned to my bed beneath his thin but tall body. He moves on top of me, grinding, and his hands roam over my chest and down my abs. One sneaks under me and squeezes my ass.

Sherlock will always be my first love, the first guy to ever touch me the way he is now, and my first heartbreak.

We're making the right decision. I know we are. It still sucks.

"Mm, I want you," he moans in my ear.

We've become experts this past year at frotting, handjobs, and blowjobs, but we haven't taken it further.

I look up into his striking green eyes. "Do you mean, like, you know …"

My soon-to-be ex-boyfriend chuckles. "Your mom might be right. If you can't even say the word *sex*, maybe you shouldn't be having it."

He's so … Sherlock.

We're totally the opposite to how we should be.

Sherlock, much like his name suggests, is smart, Wharton bound, a math genius, and a bit of a nerd. He has height, but his floppy red hair and freckles can't hide the nerdiness. Yet, when it comes to this stuff—the sex stuff—he's confident and open, and I feel like an inexperienced loser. Which is weird, because we both admitted we've never done it before. I don't know how he's so calm and collected and I'm nervous as fuck.

"I know this will totally ruin my reputation as a badass rock star—"

Sherlock snorts.

"Okay, future badass rock star." Right now, I'm in a garage band that's going nowhere, but that's all going to change this summer. I'm heading to LA and I'm never looking back. "But, uh, I want to, and stuff—"

Sherlock reaches for my erection pressing against him. "Clearly."

I shudder under his touch as he strokes my dick.

"You like that, baby?" he whispers.

"Fuck, you know I do."

"I'm good at taking care of you."

I squeeze my eyes shut and nod.

"I could take care of you in other ways." His hand moves down my cock and cups my balls, but his fingers keep going. When he presses one against my hole, I tense. He backs off. "Or, we could do it the other way around."

"No," I blurt. "Way too much pressure. I don't want to hurt you."

"If you're doing it right, it won't hurt."

"What if I do it *wrong*? I want you … like … in me. I just …" I'm a fumbly ball of nerves.

So sexy, Cashton. Really.

"I've got you." Sherlock takes control the best way he knows how. He gets me on my hands and knees to make it easier for both of us. He's gentle and slow, and yeah, it's awkward as fuck and there's a lot of stopping and starting. But he claims me in a way no one ever has.

I have the sinking feeling no one ever will again.

Not physically but the way he loves me. The way he's tender and caring. The way I know that even though we're walking away from us, he'll forever be branded on my heart.

Tomorrow, he's moving to Philly, and in a few weeks, I'm headed for Hollywood.

I don't want to chase my dream without him, but I refuse to hold him back from his. We're eighteen. It's smart to end this now. We're too young and inexperienced to try long distance.

When he comes inside me, I know it's all over, and I let the tears fall from my eyes.

Sherlock rolls me onto my back and kisses me hard. I'm thankful he doesn't see the redness in my eyes or the wetness on my cheeks. His hand distracts me from the pain in my chest as he jerks me off, and the sensation is enough to protect me from the real world. Even if I know it's fleeting. It doesn't take him long to push me over the edge, and as he collapses on top of me, more emotion takes hold.

I realize I will forever be the douche who cried after losing his virginity.

That's not very rock star at all.

I can't hide it either, because I'm about to snot all over his shoulder. That's probably worse than the crying thing. I sniff, and Sherlock stiffens in my arms.

He leans up on his elbows and stares down into my eyes. His hand brushes my long hair off my face, and he frowns.

"What's wrong? Did I hurt you? You should've told me—"

I shake my head. "You didn't hurt me." Not physically, anyway. "I just … I hate that this is the last time."

"Technically it was the first."

I manage a laugh. "No shit, Sher—"

He covers my mouth with his hand. "Cashton Alexis Kingsley. Don't finish that."

He hates his name with a passion, and I can't say I blame him. I have no idea what his parents were thinking.

Me, I wasn't given a middle name, so last year, Sherlock decided he'd make one up for me. It changes every single time.

Sherlock kisses me softly. "I'm going to miss you. So fucking much."

"Me too. Maybe I should go out to New York instead or—"

"No. LA is where you need to be."

His body leaves me, and I miss it already. When he flops onto his back next to me, I don't hesitate in cuddling up to him.

We lie there in silence, my head on his shoulder, his arm around me.

"You're going to make it," Sherlock says. "One day the name Cashton Beverly Kingsley will be everywhere. And I'll be able to say 'Yeah, I took that guy's virginity.'"

"How nice of you."

He squeezes me in a hug. "We're doing the right thing. It's the mature decision."

"I never claimed to be mature, can I take it back?"

"No."

I sigh. "I know this is the right thing, but fuck … my heart is breaking."

"Mine too," he whispers. Sherlock rolls on his side, bringing me with him so we're face-to-face. "Let's make a deal. When you're big and famous and have practically forgotten about me, we'll reconnect."

I'll jump at any chance or excuse to see him, but I'm not naïve. The chances of me actually making it are small, but I need to give myself a shot. *Trying and failing is better than not trying at all* and all that other inspirational bullshit.

"Okay, but what constitutes as big and famous? Do I, like, have to win a Grammy or something? Because I'm pretty sure we'll never see each other again if that's the basis of fame."

Sherlock purses his lips. "Hmm, no. You can be successful without a Grammy. What about ..." His eyes glimmer. "If you ever get to play Death Valley, I'll go."

"But you hate Death Valley. When I dragged you there last year, I thought we'd break up, you hated it so much. You said it was hot and gross and I quote, 'Too much desert for this ginger.'"

He grins. "All the more reason for me to go when you're there. I'll be going especially for you."

"That'll take me three years, tops." Hopefully.

"I guess I'll see you in three years, then."

"Promise?"

"To the ends of the earth."

"Sherlock, I ..." I can't swallow. My tongue is too thick. "I lo—"

"I know you do. I do too."

His lips meet mine, and I try to lock in the taste of him. His mouth is warm and soft, and he tastes like cherry from drinking Dr. Pepper.

The sound of the front door to my house closing echoes down the hall, and Sherlock pulls back, his eyes wide.

"Is that your mom—"

"Cashton, honey?"

"Fuck," we hiss and scramble to get dressed.

There's a twinge in my ass as I stand that I don't think I'll ever get used to, but it was worth it. As I watch Sherlock pull on his pants and throw his shirt over his head, I think … yeah, it was totally worth it.

But now it's tainted with the memory of him kissing me briefly and climbing out my bedroom window for the very last time.

It's done. We're over.

CHAPTER ONE
CASH

"LOOKS like you all had fun last night." The sound of Thorne's voice this early in the day is like someone stabbing me with a million tiny knives in my brain.

"Shh," Seb, my lead guitarist, says for me. We're kindred spirits.

The armchair I fell asleep on is uncomfortable ... wait ... did my hotel room have an armchair?

I crack my eyes open and move my long hair off my face. It's gotten so long lately it sits past my pecs and I can use it as a curtain over my eyes when I sleep. I slowly shift and glance around the room. High ceilings, brick walls, black floorboards, and lights. Oh, dear God, the harsh dressing room lights. "When did we get to the arena?"

My drummer, Jasper, laughs at me. "We dragged your passed-out ass here."

"Oh. Good work." I close my eyes again. "Go team."

"You might want to be awake for this," Thorne says.

I open one eye to glare at our manager. "For what?"

Thorne smiles. "I got the call. It's official. A two-hour set on the mainstage at Death Valley is yours."

"Holy shit," Greg, our bass player, exclaims. "Fuckin' really?"

Thorne, composed and immaculately dressed in a suit like he always is, says, "Fuckin' really."

The guys jump up out of their seats, suddenly forgetting their hangovers.

Mine sets in worse. I don't move. I might not even be breathing.

It's been a long journey to get here. So. Fucking. Long.

Much longer than I thought it'd be.

Years of shitty gigs after shittier self-funded tours, two steps forward, ten giant leaps back. The number of times we almost got signed to a label only to have something go wrong to make the deal fall through was heartbreaking.

When my first ever lead guitarist found out I was gay, he was out faster than any of us could say *homophobic dickweed.* Since then, we've been through a bass player leaving due to addiction and needing a break from the "scene" and a drummer who had a freak accident and lost thirty percent of feeling in his hand. He could still do regular stuff, but playing was no longer an option.

It's taken a lot of frustration and seven years of working two jobs to support our broke asses.

But it's amazing how fast everything can change in this business.

We signed with Joystar records three years ago, and since then, there's been no stopping us. The media call us insta-famous because we hit it big with our first studio album, but they don't take into account all the indie albums we put out or the shit we had to go through to get there. They don't know about the countless nights I contemplated giving up and going home.

Selfishly—and stupidly—I wanted to prove I could do it. I knew I had the talent and the drive, but that's not a guarantee in this business. You need more.

And maybe proving myself has nothing to do with the industry and everything to do with a certain boy I haven't spoken to in eight years.

Eight. Fucking. Years.

His junior year of college, Sherlock went dark. I never did work out if he blocked me on every social media platform known to man or if he deleted all of his accounts. I messaged some high school friends, but Sherlock being the nerd genius he was, people barely remembered him even existing let alone knew what he was doing two years past graduating.

"I think he's gone catatonic." Seb clicks his fingers in front of my face.

"Wha?" I sound dazed, but hey, let's chalk that up to last night's activities instead of the haunting memories of Sherlock Emerson and the pact we made the last night we ever saw each other.

"Maybe he's stroking out?" Jasper says.

I shake it off. "I'm not stroking out. This is fucking huge." Bigger than huge but for different reasons than the guys'.

Seb pulls me up and takes me into a hug. "This is next-level, man."

I hold on tight in fear of falling back down. "It's … crazy."

"Anything that renders you speechless is," Thorne says.

I step out of Seb's arms. "Yeah, yeah, yeah."

Thorne claps once. "All right, Cash, go shower and wake up properly. Boys, get ready for the meet and greet."

"Wait, what time is it?" I look around the room. "What city are we in again?"

Everyone laughs.

Thorne grips my shoulder. "Maybe lay off the alcohol for a while?"

That doesn't answer my questions but whatever.

Thorne pushes me toward the bathroom. "Go."

"Fine," I mumble.

Under the spray, I moan at the heat beating down on my tired muscles. My long hair falls in my face, and it's due for a good shampoo, but I'll cover it in product to make it look permanently wet and wash it back at the hotel tonight.

I lather myself in soap, washing away the hangover, and begin to feel half human again.

Maybe Thorne is right and I need to take a break from all the partying. I'm not as bad as some in this industry—I tend to steer clear of the hard stuff like drugs after seeing our old bass player go through addiction—but it's true what they say about being a rock star. Partying is the type of lifestyle I signed up for. It's everywhere. It's the culture.

It's amazing.

I rub my temples to soothe my aching head.

It's *mostly* amazing.

I close my eyes and mutter to myself, "Definitely taking a break."

Even if the mere thought of performing at Death Valley and the possibility of seeing Sherlock after all this time makes me want to drink.

The part of my heart where Sherlock lives beats differently to the rest. It flutters in anticipation at the thought of him coming to a gig. I gave up a long time ago thinking it'd happen. I knew it was impossible, but for the first few shows I ever played, even though they were in crappy dive bars, I always kept an eye out for him. Illogical because he was across the country, but it didn't stop me from fantasizing.

Every. Time.

That vanished when he literally disappeared. One day he was the guy liking my statuses, tweets, and Instagram pics, and the next he fell off the face of the planet.

When I called his mom, her homophobic ass told me he needed space away from people like *me*. Like three thousand miles wasn't enough.

So I gave him space.

Eight years of it.

But now it's time for him to come home.

It's time for both of us.

I shut off the shower before I get too wallow-y and try to shake off the sickly feeling in my gut. I don't know if it's from the hangover or from thinking about *him*.

I don't let myself think about him because even though we decided years ago we were doing the right thing, it has always felt *wrong*.

Hooking up with other guys has always left me with a sense of guilt and emptiness. My body's there for it, but my mind is somewhere else. Trying to have relationships is even worse. I can never give myself fully when I've always belonged to someone else. So I don't even try anymore.

I wrap my lower half in a towel and open the door to find Thorne holding up my least favorite pair of leather pants.

"No," I complain.

"They make your ass look great."

"They cut off circulation to my balls."

"It's not like you're going to reproduce anyway." He throws them at me.

"How homophobic of you. Lots of gay people are parents."

"I meant that because you're *you*, not because you're gay, asshole."

"Yes, my asshole is very gay."

"Get dressed already."

I huff and then start the arduous task of slipping into these pants. I try jumping, getting on the floor and wiggling them up my legs, and when all that doesn't work, I kick around and hope for a miracle.

The guys find my struggle hilarious, but none of them come to try and help me.

"I hate you all." I grunt.

Seb's the one to come to my rescue.

He gets me off the ground and tells me to hold on to the doorframe of the bathroom. His big, guitar-playing hands yank the pants up, but they move maybe an inch.

At least they're up to my thighs now.

By the time they're finally in place, we're both sweaty and breathing heavy.

"Was it good for you?" Seb slaps my shoulder.

I shove him away from me. "Not even a little bit. Which I'm sure you've heard a lot."

He waggles his fingers. "Whatever. These are magic."

"I'll take your word for it."

We have one rule in our band: no fucking around with each other. Pretty easy for Greg and Jasper, the straight boys. Seb and I agreed early on not to get involved in band drama. The music always comes first.

I know some acts do their VIP meet and greets after their show, but we like to get it out of the way. After the set is for relaxing and partying. By that time, I'm done being *on*.

It means we have to be at the arena stupidly early, like

midafternoon. That's still the middle of the goddamn night if you ask me.

I slip on a black button-up but leave it undone, run some product through my long messy hair, apply a thin layer of eyeliner, and then turn to everyone. "Done."

"You're so pretty," Jasper says, and I flip him off.

We take our time meeting with fans and taking photos, but my head's not in it. The guys pick up the slack for me, doing most of the talking and charming everyone.

I can fake smiles and answer questions, but my personality is flat.

At one point, Seb leans in close. "Why are you being weird?"

"Why are you being weird?" I bite.

"I'm always weird."

"True."

"You're not ... yourself."

"And what is myself?"

"Lively. Happy. A pain in the ass. You're not quiet."

Sebastian came into my life after I'd given up on Sherlock. He's my best friend, and there isn't much I don't tell him. But Sherlock ... I don't speak about him. Most days, I pretend he doesn't exist, just like his internet presence.

"We'll talk later?"

He throws his arm around my shoulder for a photo. "Pull it together, man."

I do. Mostly.

It's not until we're stage side, ready to go on, that it hits me again.

I flash back to those first few years without *him*. I ran a blog called *Operation: Death Valley*. It basically documented the highs and lows of trying to make it in the biz, all with the end goal of making it to the festival where my high school love and I had agreed to meet.

I kept it going for a year after Sherlock disappeared.

Then I got mad and deleted it all.

And now the opportunity to go to Death Valley is here. Seven years later than I thought I would be.

I stare out at the packed stadium of tonight's show. Our current tour is going well, and our fan base is growing daily. Our singles regularly hit number one in rock on iTunes, and as soon as this tour's over, we're going to be cutting our third studio album. Two albums in three years have been pushing us and working us until we're bone-tired, but right now … this moment …

"Ever experience one of those times where you realize everything you've been working for is right in front of you?" I blurt out.

My bandmates look at me as if I'm crazy.

To be fair, if I'm only now realizing we're famous, I might be a little slow. But it's the first time I've actually thought … *Holy shit. This is my life now.*

I've finally made it.

I just don't know if it's too late for Sherlock.

THE CIRCULAR PIECE of metal spins on top of the glass table in front of me until it falls on its side.

I pick it up and spin it again.

Spin, spin, spin.

"I think that's the last of it." Shannon walks into the kitchen and takes a bottle of water out of the practically empty fridge. "No regrets?"

I glance up at them. They came into my life when I really needed someone. They taught me a lot just by being themself. I'm not nonbinary like them, but they gave me power in owning who I am to my core.

I have a lot of regrets, but knowing them isn't one of them. "Nope. You?"

"Nah." They smile and take their phone out of their pocket. "I have something for you, though. Think of it as a parting gift."

"Why am I scared suddenly?"

The phone appears in front of me with a headline that stops my heart dead.

Cash Me Outside Signs on for Death Valley Music Festival.

"Isn't that the band you've stalked since before I even met you?" Shannon asks.

"Stalking is definitely not the right word."

Checking up on, maybe. Following, definitely. Okay, so maybe stalking *is* the right word.

"You check every single year if they're going to be there."

I frown up at them. "How do you know I'm not looking for a different band?"

"Name one other rock band."

"Umm …" Why can I not think of any? I know tons. Like … shit.

"Exactly. You should go."

"I'm not going to go." I stand to leave, but Shannon stops me, their perfectly manicured hand catching my forearm.

"Why not?"

"There's something you don't know. About me."

Their hand releases me, and those stormy gray eyes I've stared into for the past two and a half years narrow. "You're a closeted ex-rock star and there was a big feud between your band and Cash Me Outside where you had to fake your death and leave that scene forever?"

I touch my hand to my heart. "How do you know me so far deep in my soul you could've guessed that?"

"What are ex-spouses for?" They wink.

I wince.

"Too soon?" they ask.

"Way too soon."

Though that's not entirely true. In all truth, Shannon and I have been separated longer than we were even married.

That's what happens when you have an existential crisis,

make impulsive decisions, and then take on a life mantra to seize the day. Carpe diem and all that crap.

Wham, bam, marriage license signed.

And then a year later, *hello, divorce proceedings.*

It all happened that fast.

Shannon takes me over to the living room in the hotel suite my boss has let me rent until I'm back on my feet. They force me to sit on the plush couch, and I'm only mildly worried about what kind of bodily fluids I'm sitting in. This is Vegas after all.

"What don't I know about you?" Shannon asks.

"Cashton …"

"As in Cash Kingsley? Rock god and fucking sex on a stick?"

I nod. "You know where his hometown is?"

"Isn't he from Boulder City like you?"

"Know how old he is?"

"I'm gonna go out on a limb here and say around your age?"

"Wanna know how many high schools are in Boulder City?"

Get there faster, Shannon.

Realization dawns. "Oh. You and him …"

"We were each other's firsts."

"Aww, how … oddly cool is it that I've technically slept with Cash Kingsley? In a roundabout way."

I start a slow clap. "And look at that! Making it about yourself."

They don't even care. They flip their long dark hair. "Always."

"So, what, Cash is back in the same state as you in how

many years, and you're going to skip seeing him? Did it end on bad terms?"

I laugh. "No. It ended … perfectly."

"Come on. I can't even win best breakup in your life?"

I level them with a look.

"Right. Made it about me again. Sorry. Continue."

"We made a stupid pact."

That's the thing that gets me the most. This is either the crappiest timing for Cash to be at Death Valley or the best it could've ever been.

I let out a humorless laugh.

"What was the pact?" Shannon asks.

"That if Cashton ever made it to Death Valley, I'd go watch him play and we'd reconnect."

Shannon's eyes widen. "No shit. Really? Do you not see how perfect this is?"

"Shan, it's so much more complicated than that."

"What makes it complicated?"

"I haven't spoken to him in eight years."

"Why not?"

"I …" I shake my head. "I don't think it matters. He won't forgive the way I cut him out of my life. Fuck, either that or he probably doesn't even remember me. He's a *rock star*. Imagine how many guys he's fucked since me."

"No one could ever forget you, Locke."

I snort. "He doesn't even know I changed my name."

"Then it sounds like you have a lot to catch up on. You should go."

I know I promised to go, but I don't know if I can handle it.

When Cashton and I parted ways, I spent my first two years in school trying to forget about him. That was impossible when all I'd do is stalk him on social media.

It's why I had to block him. No, not just block him but delete my online life completely.

I had to live a normal college experience. Go to parties. Date. I needed to be the grown-up I promised him I'd be when we broke up.

I told myself if he didn't make it to Death Valley by the time I got my MBA, I'd reach out to him and explain my absence.

I figured I had a few years to get being young out of my system, and then I'd go back to Cashton.

The closer graduation loomed, the more excitement bubbled in my gut, along with a sense of dread.

What if we weren't the same people anymore? What if he'd fallen into the world of rock and either drank, snorted, or shot up so many times he wasn't my Cashton anymore?

What if he didn't like the person I'd become? Or … not become. I was exactly the same person I was when I'd left high school with marginally more dating experience.

And then? A few short months before my hooding ceremony, Cash Me Outside exploded. Everywhere.

That made me want to contact him even more, but when I went looking for all his old social media profiles, I realized they were all deleted. It made sense. He was a superstar now, so he'd have PR-controlled accounts.

When I looked those up, I thought about the thousands of people who must be randomly messaging him. The thousands of fans who'd want him for being famous.

I'd just be another person wanting him for what he was, not who he is.

We'd agreed that when he made it big, we'd catch up, but in the moment, it felt like I'd only be contacting him because of his fame.

I didn't want that.

I might have always appeared confident around Cashton, but it was all an act. I was faking it. I wasn't sure I could have faked it anymore.

Seeing him in tabloids with other celebrities, seeing his rumored love life in countless online articles, I realized how different we were.

How different we always were.

I was sure that even if we were to get back in touch, those differences in our personalities would no longer be cute like they were in high school.

That's when I turned down my graduate offers for employment and took a gap year. I traveled. I did wild shit.

I backpacked across Europe, slung beers, partied, and saw the world.

Fell in love.

Or … lust.

Fell in … companionship. That's probably the best word for it.

I do love Shannon, but as two Americans who randomly met in Greece, fell in love in Germany, and got married in the Netherlands, it was all a crazy whirlwind that probably shouldn't have happened.

What seemed like a great idea at the time was an already tension-filled mistake by the time we got back Stateside.

Not to mention the long-ass divorce that followed with complications from an international marriage of two American citizens.

Dated a few weeks. Married for a year. Separated for eighteen months.

Hell, I'd still be living with them if my boss at Catalina

Resort and Casino on the Strip hadn't heard my story and offered this room for as long as I needed it.

It's not much, but it has a combined living and dining room, small kitchen, and a bedroom with a nice view and jacuzzi tub in the corner.

This is just another mess I'd have to explain to Cashton if I were to go to Death Valley.

If he was even interested. If he even remembers the pact.

It's been ten years.

"What famous rock star would remember the nerdy numbers guy from high school?" I say more to myself.

Shannon leans in. "What guy forgets who he lost his virginity to?"

Point taken.

They nudge me with their shoulder. "You should go."

I should.

But I know I won't.

DEEP BREATH, Cash.

I haven't experienced these kind of nerves since my first live performance at the VMAs. There's a lot riding on this festival. Not only for my career but my life.

I've waited for this moment since Sherlock climbed out my window over a decade ago.

"You should've contacted him," Seb says beside me.

After the show where we got the news we'd be performing here, I let it all out to the guys.

Seb thinks not tracking him down is stupid because I'm putting all my hopes into the notion that this guy will remember a pact he made when he was eighteen years old right after he'd busted a nut inside me. He thinks I'm setting myself up for disappointment, and I'd be lying if I said I hadn't thought the exact same thing.

But I haven't had the guts to reach out to the stranger he now is. And other than trying to find his parents, who didn't want to help me get in contact with him years ago or someone else from our old life who might know where he is, I wouldn't know where to look anyway.

From what I can find online, Sherlock Emerson doesn't exist anymore.

The ball is in his court.

And in my throat.

I swallow hard around the lump. "Can't you tell me he'll turn up, he'll be the same sweet guy I remember from high school, and I'll fulfill a lifelong dream and live happily ever after?"

Seb purses his lips. "Tell me again how you're not getting your hopes up?"

He's right. He's so right.

The chance of Sherlock actually being here right now, out in the bright sun and desert heat, just waiting for me to take the stage is slim.

He's not out there. He's *not*.

Yet, as we're led from our tour bus to the stage for our set, I'm constantly glancing around the grounds, checking every face for the older version of the boy I once loved, and I'm really regretting my decision to be sober for this.

Thorne was right that I needed a break from the partying.

Instead, I've been throwing all my energy into putting on the best show of Death Valley.

All for him.

A guy who is most likely never going to show up.

I've been looking out for him for days. The headliners play the final day of the festival, and while there hasn't been any reason for Sherlock to come early considering this wasn't his thing, I thought maybe he might be here.

But all I've seen are unfamiliar faces in the crowds of people here for the music. Not love.

I keep forgetting the real point of Death Valley.

This was once my dream, and now all I dream about is a redheaded boy from my past.

"Play it cool," Seb says. "Desperation doesn't look good on a rock star."

"I can make anything look good."

"If you say so."

Yet, even as I say the words, I don't feel them.

I'm shirtless, lathered up in so much sunblock it looks like I'm covered in oil, and I've got these damn chains around my neck that drape over my chest. They look cool, but they weigh me down and sit uncomfortably on my skin and I'm sure my hair is going to get tangled in them at some point.

At least Thorne let me wear my fake leather pants today— the ones that have stretch in them. Wearing real leather in this heat might kill me.

"Are you really going to make us do the song?" Seb asks.

"Yes. We're doing the song."

"If I haven't told you lately, I hate you."

"Agreed," Jasper and Greg say behind us.

"It's one song."

"It's a Katy Perry song," Seb reminds me.

"You're gay. You're supposed to love her."

Behind me, the straight dudes snicker.

Thorne catches up to us, but his face doesn't give me the warm and fuzzies I was expecting.

"Anything?" I ask.

He shakes his head.

I left two tickets at will call for Sherlock. Two, because I wanted to be nice in case he wanted to bring someone.

A friend.

Not a boyfriend.

God, I hope he doesn't have a boyfriend.

My stomach sours.

I wonder what he's been up to all these years. What he's been doing. *Who* he's been doing.

I haven't been a monk, not by a long shot, but by rock star standards, I'm lacking quite a few notches on my bedpost.

I realized how much Sherlock had been holding me back in that department when I had a fling with my producer. An ex-boy bander who said I was even more emotionally unavailable than he was, and that's bad.

My heart has always belonged to someone I don't know anymore.

Knowing Sherlock hasn't picked up the tickets I left for him plants the first real thoughts of doubt inside me.

I've been trying to tell myself he isn't coming, but I've always believed in my heart that he would.

Now, I'm not so sure. We're about to go on, and he's only got the next two hours to get here or he'll miss it.

There are two songs especially for him that I worked into this set.

I ask Thorne to keep checking the tickets for me, but he refuses. Something about not wanting to keep running back to the front gates every five minutes to aid in getting me some sex.

So not what this is about, but whatever. I'm not getting into it with him. Or either of the other guys.

"Please, welcome to the stage, Cash Me Outside!"

We rush up to our positions, and I scream into the mic. "How shitfaced is everyone?"

I knew the reaction was going to be loud, but fuck … I'll be lucky to hear the music even with my earpiece in.

Seb and I share a smile as waves of excitable energy pulse

outward from the crowd and are sent our way. The atmosphere of a live show is the best thing in the world. Nothing beats it.

"Good," Seb says into his own mic. "The more fucked-up you are, the better we sound."

Jasper starts the intro to our latest hit on his drums, and I close my eyes and let the beat flow through me. It vibrates in my chest, as if my heart is following Jasper's rhythm.

Greg joins in on bass.

Then Seb rips into the opening chords on his guitar.

We start with a bang of pyrotechnics exploding from the stage like a wall of fire surrounding us, and the audience's anticipation of everything that's about to come out my mouth settles the nerves inside me.

I was born to do this. This was always going to be my destiny, and I wouldn't trade it for the world. But out there, somewhere in this crowd, I hope there's the man I loved enough once upon a time to consider it.

I add the intentional rasp into my voice with the opening lines.

Bleeding heart
  Torn apart

The crowd eats it up, and this is why I do what I do. For moments like this. I own the stage and every single person listening to me.

But as we work through the songs on our set list, and I strut across the stage and do my thing, the closer we get to that inevitable moment where we're due to leave the stage.

I can't help wondering if Sherlock will be there waiting for me.

The more I think about him not being there, the more strained my voice becomes. Even to the point where Seb takes a time-out between songs under the proviso to get a drink of water. He brings it over to me.

"Forget about him, man. Focus on what's in front of you."

I've been doing that for ten years to try to get here.

This is supposed to be the end of all accomplishments.

I stare out into the crowd, looking for a head of ginger hopefully sticking out under the desert sun.

There're too many people. They're all packed into the cordoned-off desert like sardines.

He could be anywhere.

Or nowhere.

Seb's right. I need to forget about him and focus.

If he's here, he deserves the best performance of my life.

If he's not, the fans deserve the same amount of energy as Sherlock does.

I steal Seb's water.

He doesn't even care.

I sing my heart out for the rest of the songs on the set list, and then we reach the new one. One no one has ever heard before.

It's been ten years
   Since I saw your face
   Wanting to talk to you
   Wanting to see this through

Ten years
  Countless beers
  Missing you forever
  Always losing my nerve
  I want to hold you
  To the ends of the earth.

I can tell we lose some of the crowd, but I don't care. This song isn't for them. This is for the boy I fell hard for at seventeen years old. Said goodbye to at eighteen. And for the man he now is. Whoever that may be.

In my mind, he graduated from Wharton and went on to be some big, important CFO of some company somewhere.

He's still the same Sherlock. Nerdy on the outside, a confident toppy guy on the inside.

We've saved our biggest hit for last, so that's okay, but I don't know how well they're going to react to a Katy Perry song—rock version.

Seb gives me the *you owe me* look right before addressing the crowd. "Don't judge us for this next one. We lost a bet."

I flip him off, and the crowd goes wild.

There's a reason for Katy Perry. I'm not a closeted pop wannabe.

It just so happens the year this song came out was the same year Sherlock and I started dating. With the amount of airtime it got, it always reminds me of him.

And when we start singing "Teenage Dream," surprisingly, the crowd goes even wilder. They start singing along to the point I don't have to sing at all.

Who knew Katy Perry would be such a big hit at a rock festival? I side glance at Seb, and he looks as confused as I am.

We shrug it off and keep rocking out to a song whose target demographic is teenage girls.

It's actually a lot of fun, but I'll never, ever admit that out loud. I have a big rock star image to protect.

When we kick into the last song, the screams are deafening. This baby hit the charts and got played to death across radio stations and streaming services.

That cheering. That kind of fandom. This is what musicians live for.

I invoke the rock persona, leaning forward with both hands wrapped around the microphone while I belt out the lyrics.

My hips move, I shake my ass, and I work the stage like a stripper minus the pole. And, uh, the stripping part. Although, I am practically naked already.

Pretty sure anyone in the front can see my dick print through my pants.

When Seb joins in on the chorus, I approach him, and we stand back to back.

Jasper isn't as comfortable with the grinding up on him thing, which is why I stick to doing it to Seb. It makes the tabloids think something is going on between us, because, you know, two gay guys knowing each other without boning is impossible.

We don't exactly dispel the rumors, but that's a marketing ploy more than anything else.

If it were true, we're the worst boyfriends ever. We cheat on each other. A lot.

When the song finishes, all four of us are breathing heavy.

We say thank you and wish the crowd a great festival, and only when we leave the stage do I let myself think of Sherlock again.

I glance out at the crowd, at all the faces lining the barricades trying to get our attention.

I wave but don't see who I'm looking for.

"Great set," Thorne says.

"Did he—"

"I was too busy watching you guys rock it. Who would've thought your biggest song of the night would be a Katy Perry song?"

"I feel like we should be offended at that," Seb says.

Jasper throws his arm around me as we head away from the stage and walk toward our tour bus. "Who fucking cares. They loved it, that's the main thing. We're gonna go get a drink. You in?"

I glance at Thorne.

He knows what I want. "I'll go check the ticket booth again."

"I'll be in the bus. You guys go have fun."

We break off in three different directions, and I'm thankful the guys are leaving me to my own devices.

I trudge through the desert to the backstage area where all the tour busses are parked and climb the steps of ours.

My first stop is the mini fridge.

Ignoring all the Dr. Pepper I ordered for *him,* I grab a beer and go sit at the little table to wait for the bad news.

Because it has to be bad news.

If he was here, I would've seen him by now, right?

The text comes through a few minutes later.

Thorne: *Tickets are still at will call. Sorry, Cash. I know you really wanted it.*

I didn't know it was possible, but it's as if my heart is breaking all over again. Eighteen-year-old me is sitting under the surface of my now harder features, threatening to bubble to the surface. Just like the night he walked away from me, the night he stood me up from a decade-long promise will mark itself in my chest as the second time Sherlock Emerson broke my heart.

I hold up my beer. "Cheers to heartbreak."

The very mature plan is to get as hammered as everyone out in that desert, but on my second beer, there's a loud rapping on the tour bus door.

It's fucking open, shitheads.

They couldn't have gotten so wasted in the short time since I left them they don't realize the door is open, right?

There's another knock and a deep voice I don't know. "Mr. Kingsley?"

With a furrowed brow, I climb out from behind the table and stumble toward the door.

A huge security guard blocks the entrance. "There's a guy here saying you're expecting him, but he doesn't have a backstage pass. Your manager said it's okay, but I wanted to be sure."

My heart stops dead.

Literally dead.

I'm dead, aren't I?

I wasn't on beer number two like I thought but beer number two hundred. I'm collapsed in my own pile of spew and dying slowly of liver failure or something.

Yet, when the security guy steps aside and a face I haven't seen in forever fills the space, I know with certainty that I'm not fantasizing or dying or any of that.

No alcohol-induced dreaming could conjure someone so goddamn hot.

He still has his red hair, but it's lighter and shiny like a strawberry blond. It's swept back with product and looks silky smooth. He's wearing a crisp light gray three-piece suit with a royal blue tie.

He's the most beautiful man I've ever seen in my life, and my mouth dries.

"You're here," I croak.

His smile is so much more grown-up.

All of him looks the same but more distinguished.

"May I come up?"

How is it possible his voice got even deeper?

Fuck. My cock strains against my tight pleather pants.

I nod.

He turns to the security guard and thanks him, but as he climbs the three steps, I have to force myself to step back. Because if he comes anywhere near me, the only catching up we'll be doing is of the naked kind.

Only, he doesn't stop. He follows me farther into the bus with a predatory look in his eye.

"Sherlock?" I rasp.

"Cashton Rosaline Kingsley." I'm engulfed in his surprisingly toned arms. He used to be all skin and bones. Now he's got some meat on him. "I'm home, baby."

Holy. Shit.

I COULDN'T NOT COME. I had to at least see him perform.

I've seen countless songs and concert clips on YouTube, but nothing—*nothing*—beats the real thing.

The plan was to watch him, maybe catch his eye and see if there's any spark of recognition, but I couldn't get remotely close to the stage.

Then it was too hot, so I moved to where pop-up tents were set up to get out of the sun.

Fucking ginger gene.

Still, I hadn't decided if I was going to try to talk to him afterward or not. Or if I'd even be allowed.

I was fully waiting for security to tell me I'm shit out of luck, but apparently, they'd been told of my possible arrival by Cashton's manager.

I huff.

Manager.

Cashton has come so far, and until the moment I saw him, until we came face-to-face, I didn't know how I'd respond to being in his presence again.

Apparently my first response was to wrap myself around him and call him a term of endearment I have no right in using anymore.

"I've missed you," I rumble in his ear. It's clear I have no control over my mouth at all.

He smells different. He feels different. More man and less … boy.

Even though he was eighteen the last time I saw him and not much different to now.

He's just … different. But I love it instead of despising it like I was worried I would.

He's lived a long ten years, and I want to know every story, every adventure, but he's frozen against me, and now it's becoming abundantly clear that this is probably crossing a whole heap of lines.

I pull back but can't help keeping my arms around him. "Cashton?"

His brown eyes blink up at me. His hair has gotten even longer than the last time I saw him, bringing back the eighties rock band look, and his tempting mouth I've missed so much is only inches away. Nope, closer than that.

Closer.

His tongue darts out, wetting his lip.

"Cashton …" I say again.

"Fuck it, we can catch up later." He closes the small gap between us, pressing his mouth to mine.

Pressing, attaching, attacking … Same thing, right?

Damn, I remember everything about the way this man kisses. I remember his demanding tongue that liked to dominate my mouth, right up until I fought back and took control of it. Of everything.

Of his tongue, his mouth, his body …

The moan he lets out is deep and guttural, and worry about crossing lines is no longer at the forefront of my mind.

I'm still taller than him, but he used to be more muscular than me. Neither of us look like muscly gym rats, but I've at least filled out enough to match him in that area now. It makes me feel bigger than him, probably bigger than I actually am, but fitting myself against him, I surround him and hold him to me as if he was always mine to possess.

Cashton trembles in my arms the way he used to. The way he would when he wanted something but was too shy to ask for it.

"I want you to fuck me," he demands.

Guess that shy thing is something he got over, then.

As much as I should pull away and slow this down, there's no way that's possible.

"Turn around." My throat is scratchy and dry, putting an extra growl in my voice.

Like any time I'd told Cashton to do something in bed, he complies immediately.

Nostalgia settles over me.

I plaster my front to his back and push him toward the side of the bus. Only when I get him into position—his hands on the windows with his ass sticking out—do I ease up on him.

His narrow hips feel amazing in my hands, and that round butt of his looks amazing framed in those tight pants.

"I've fucking missed this ass." I press forward, rubbing against him with my already hard and aching cock.

Cashton moans. "I've missed your dick."

I find that hard to believe when I'm sure he's had a buffet of cocks since the one and only time I fucked him, but now's not the time to get into that.

I'm going to take his words at face value—that he's missed

my cock now it's pressed against him.

I run my hand down the middle of his back, and he shudders under my touch. "You gonna take me like you did ten years ago? Want me to fuck you until you can't shake your ass onstage like I saw today? You think this ass belongs to your *fans*?"

"Well, it hasn't belonged to you in ten years."

I try not to wince. Instead, I take on that commanding, dominant role I know he loved even back then. I want to show him that even though so long has passed, I'm not all that different. I still want him crumbling for me and coming apart from my touch, my mouth, my body.

My fist tangles in his long hair, and he yelps in pain, but I don't let up. "I have news for you. It has *always* belonged to me."

"Then where the fuck you been?" he spits out.

That's a loaded question.

Just like he lied about missing my cock, I slap his ass and do the same. "Been dreaming about this." I spank him again, and he moans. "You gonna let me in there?"

All he does is nod.

"Take off your pants," I order.

As he pops the button on his pants, he glances at me over his shoulder and smirks.

There's the boy I used to love.

Still love.

Might love again one day.

I've been in his presence for mere minutes, and my head's already floating in the clouds.

I shake it off.

He pulls his pants down to his knees and then doesn't bother with taking them off. He doesn't need to.

He's gone commando, so he's all bare and ready for me.

"Bend over."

Cash widens his feet as much as his pants allow him to, and he bends at the waist.

I bite my fist to stop the feral noises from escaping or from me blurting out something that this whole thing isn't about.

I don't know what this hookup is about, but I don't want to bring that up now by saying something stupid like *"You're perfect."*

Movement outside catches my eye, but it's only someone walking by and heading toward the stages. It scares me enough to ask, "Your bandmates aren't going to come in here at any moment, are they?"

"I don't fucking care if they do. They've seen me in worse positions than this."

Not exactly what I want to visualize right now, but with one plea from him, I'm back in the game.

"Just please hurry up. Please."

I lean over him. "Mm, I like it when you beg."

He shudders again.

"Stay there and stand still. You're not allowed to move an inch. Got it?"

He mumbles something that sounds like an affirmative.

I stand upright and pull out my wallet which I'd put travel lube and a condom in—just in case. This wasn't the plan when I decided to see him at Death Valley, but I'm thankful for my need to be prepared.

Cashton flinches at the sound of my belt buckle as I loosen my pants, but apart from that, he stays completely still while I take my cock out of the hole in my underwear and suit up.

I squirt some lube onto my fingers and the rest on my dick.

Cashton watches me over his shoulder again, and I can't help smiling as I catch him checking out my cock.

"It's the same as the last time you saw it."

"What, no piercings?" he asks.

"Do I look like a piercings kind of guy?"

"Hmm, I guess not. Do I?" Cashton raises an eyebrow at me.

Holy fuck, he has a dick piercing now?

Wrapping my arm around him, my fingers encircle his thick cock and stroke him from tip to base.

He breathes heavy, and his back muscles spasm.

I explore his cock, trying to find the piece of metal.

When he laughs, I want to be mad, I really do. But I can't be.

"You don't have a piercing, do you?"

"Nope."

"You know, you don't have to trick me into touching your dick."

"Well, if you're not gonna let me touch it …"

"Fuck, you're a brat."

"Always was. Are you going to fuck me or not?"

Damn, I could get used to this version of him. I loved being the one in charge, the one to make him feel comfortable when he wasn't sure what to do, but this confident, more experienced Cashton is working for me too.

So long as I don't think too hard about where the confidence came from or the experiences he's had.

I stroke his cock while my lubed fingers press against his hole, teasing him until he loosens up enough to let one in.

His ass clenches and releases around my finger, and I can't wait to feel it on my dick.

I push a second finger in, and he calls out. Expertly, I work him open as fast as I can.

The whimpers and impatient noises falling from his mouth should be illegal. He pushes back onto my fingers, fucking himself on me, and I don't know how much longer I can take it before my dick cries from jealousy.

"Now," he pleads. "Right now."

Cashton is desperate and right where I want him, but I can't help drawing it out.

"Say please," I demand, fully expecting him to tell me to fuck off.

Instead, he turns his head, his brown eyes looking up at me with complete trust and desperation. "*Please.*"

I am so screwed.

Leaning over him, I remove my fingers from his ass and line up my cock. My mouth lands next to his ear. "Don't worry. I won't tell anyone that underneath your big, badass rock star persona, you're a cock slut just begging for my dick."

Cashton hangs his head. "Tell everyone. I don't fucking care. Just hurry up and put me out of my misery. I want to feel all of you."

I kiss his shoulder. "Anything for you."

Standing straighter, I grip his hip in one hand, my cock in the other, and I guide myself inside him.

Immediately, he becomes putty in my hands.

He shivers when I slowly push all the way in while I massage his lower back and give him time to adjust.

I let him take the lead momentarily, letting him move his hips and take me at a pace he's okay with. I have to grit my teeth to hold on to any sense of control until I'm able to move inside with ease.

He's tight and hot, and as I stare down at where we're

connected, watching as I slowly move in and out of him, I've never seen a hotter sight.

Ever.

With an experimental thrust, I slam inside him and pause, waiting for the protest that doesn't come.

"Sherlock, fuck. Do it again."

I do as he says and don't stop there.

Cashton's fingers flex on the glass in front of him, his nails going white at the tips as if he's trying to hold on to the slippery surface.

I wrap my arm around him and hold the sexy chains he wore onstage to his chest so if he does lose his grip on the window, he doesn't put his head through it.

The pressure surrounding my cock doesn't let up, just takes me higher and higher as our bodies meet over and over again until we're both sweaty, trembling, and fighting the brink of orgasm.

"You need a hand?" I grunt. "Or are you going to come hands-free because you want to make me happy?"

He gives an inarticulate answer I can only take as an affirmative, but I can't be sure.

My rhythm cracks the tiniest bit as I let out a growl. "Fuck, Cashton."

The confident and dominating voice I've been using slips back to teenage me—the one who seemed like he was put together but really wasn't.

The one who thought being mature and separating was the smart thing to do when it very well could be the worst mistake I've ever made.

I've missed Cashton. I've missed all of him.

We'd never had sex this rough, this consuming, before, and

yet being inside him still feels like I'm coming home after a long time away.

His ass clenches around my dick, and his breathing becomes shallow and stinted. "I'm gonna …"

"Do it," I breathe. Suddenly, I'm the one begging now.

Cashton throws his head back, and cum shoots out of his untouched cock, hitting me on my forearm across his chest.

I push that tiny bit harder, thrust that tiny bit faster, until I'm shuddering and filling the condom.

My fingers dig into his skin so hard he mutters something about bruises, and I have to force myself to let up while I continue to pump into him, riding out the most intense orgasm of my life.

When I finally slow down, Cashton's body turns to jelly, and I pull out of him. I find a trash can near the front of the bus and ditch the condom, tucking myself away in the process.

"My Sherlock," he murmurs when I approach him again.

I'll always be his Sherlock. Only, that's not even my name anymore.

He's still standing in the same position, and if I had the refractory period of my eighteen-year-old self, I'd want to go again. He has red marks from my hands on his hips, a used, slippery hole I want to fill again, and he's still bent over in a way I could take erotic photos right now and have material for my spank bank for life.

What was he saying?

Oh. Right. Name.

"Uh, about that …"

Cashton straightens and turns to me.

My voice is croaky as I lay my confession out here. "I go by Locke now."

His brown eyes blink at me until he realizes what I'm saying.

He pulls up his pants as fast as humanly possible. *"Locke?"*

"You know I've always hated my name." I shrug. "So, I changed it. Legally."

"When?" The question isn't angry, per se, but he's not going to be throwing me a new-name party anytime soon.

"Before I graduated Wharton. I wanted my new name on all my certificates."

It's as if I can see the millions of questions running through his head now our minds aren't clouded by sex.

"We might need to talk about a few things," I say.

Cashton folds his arms across his naked chest. "No fucking shit."

This. This was the reaction I was expecting when we met up again.

If he hadn't killed so many brain cells partying it up the rock star way and hadn't forgotten me, I knew he'd have a problem with how I handled things eight years ago when I cut him out of my life completely.

I made what I thought was the right choice—the only choice.

When someone messes up, they have to face the consequences sooner or later, and my time has come.

Instead of yelling or getting right into it, Cashton approaches me and wraps me in a hug.

I'm surprised at first, and taken aback, but I melt into him, getting lost in the familiar feeling of his slightly shorter frame.

"I'll yell at you in a minute," he says. "Right now I want you to hold me and reassure me that you're here. Please tell me this is real."

I breathe in the scent of sex and sweat and can't tell him

what he wants to hear. I'm not entirely sure this is happening. "If it's not real, I don't want it to end," I whisper.

I never thought this would happen. Cashton has been a memory impossible to live up to, but the same complete feeling I used to have with him envelops me the same way his warm arms are. It covers me like a blanket, and I never want to let go.

"I didn't think this would happen," Cashton says.

Neither did I. I didn't realize how much it needed to happen for me to see my life for the past ten years for what it was. Frivolous.

That doesn't stop me from using the jab on the tip of my tongue and turning this around on him. "It did take you a superlong time to play here."

Cashton bursts out laughing. "Asshole."

I could stand here holding him forever, but I know that's not how this is gonna go.

He pulls back and looks up at me with those dark eyes of his. "You ghosted me."

With a sigh, I let him go. "I did."

"Explain yourself."

"I'm an idiot?"

"I've known that for years. Try again."

I force a smile. "Okay. Let's do this."

LOCKE'S GREEN EYES SOFTEN. His jaw is still angular, his nose narrow, but his skin used to be pale and freckly. Now, his gorgeous freckles aren't as bright due to a light tan.

His eyes graze over me from my shirtless torso to my tight pants, and the look on his face almost makes me want to forgive him no questions asked.

He looks lost, like a wounded puppy, and while I know none of that is my fault—*he's* the one who ghosted *me*—I can't help feeling responsible.

It's so damn mind-blowing that the man who just fucked me into oblivion is the same guy standing in front of me right now with pure fear and uncertainty on his face that this isn't real, like he could wake up at any minute.

I recognize it because that's exactly what's going on inside me right now.

"Want a drink?" I ask. I move over to the mini fridge. "You've got a choice of beer or Dr. Pepper."

Locke's face lights up. "You remembered."

"I remember everything about you, and considering your

cherry cola addiction was one of the biggest things about you when you were a teenager, there's no way I was going to forget it."

"You knew I'd come."

"I'd *hoped* you'd come." I waggle my eyebrows to be a total douche. "And I guess you did. In more ways than one."

Locke scoffs. "You're still as corny as ever."

"Always. Life's too short to be serious and sincere."

"They should put that on a Hallmark card."

Nostalgia hits with such force it throws me for a second. How we can still be the same, still play off each other, but have ten years between us?

I hand him a Dr. Pepper, our fingers brushing against each other. It's so slight, yet that spark that has always crackled between us is there still.

"Come on." Locke puts the soda down and takes my hand, leading me to the long bench seat along the wall of the bus.

We sit close, our thighs touching, and he refuses to let go of me.

"I need you to know something." Locke's thumb caresses my hand. "My first two years at Wharton were hell. Literally, all I did was study. I made one friend. I didn't go to any parties, didn't join any clubs, and I spent all my spare time online stalking my ex-boyfriend who I'd stupidly let go. Watching your posts and waiting for an update from you became my life. Waiting for you to wake up on the West Coast so you could see my good-morning message became so unhealthy I was checking my phone when I should've been focusing on classes."

I know I'm supposed to see something wrong with that, but I was the same way. "The favorite part of my days back then was talking to you online or seeing you post about exams or …" Something occurs to me. "Okay, I do remember a lot of your posts being school related. I thought you were doing it to shield me from guys you were dating or something."

"I didn't date *anyone*."

"At all?" I shriek.

"That's the point. We broke up so I could have those college experiences and you could live it up in LA without guilt. After two years, my roommate had enough of my wallowing and not going out. He made me block you for one month. After that, I was allowed to unblock you if I wanted … but …"

"But you liked it so much, you figured, hey, I'm gonna make this a permanent thing?" I sound bitter. There's nothing I can do about that. I *am* bitter.

"Not at all. I fucking hated it. But for the first time in two years, I was doing what we said we would, and I was scared if I unblocked you, I'd fall back into old patterns. The plan was to unblock you when you either got here"—he gestures around the tour bus—"or I got my MBA. One or the other."

"And when you graduated, you forgot?"

"When I graduated, I … I chickened out."

"What? Why?"

"You literally hit number one on iTunes three months before I got my MBA."

"So?"

Locke winces at my raised voice. "So I'd literally be contacting you as soon as you got famous. It felt … wrong. Like you'd think I was only after your fame or your money."

"Sher—Sorry, *Locke*. That's going to be hard to get used to." I turn sideways on the bench seat, bending my knee so I can fit. "I would never think you're after my fame."

"Deep down, I probably knew that. But I was also going

through this huge transitional time in my life. I was about to graduate, I had a few offers for jobs in my field, but all of it seemed … pointless. I'd been studying too hard for too long, and I thought it would've been different. I thought I'd feel accomplished or something. I left you to go to a top school so I could get an awesome job and earn lots of money, but it didn't feel right."

"What did feel right?"

"Nothing. I saw you, saw how far you'd come with music, and when I looked at my future with numbers, there was nothing but dread in the pit of my stomach. So, I did what any recent graduate going through an existential crisis would do."

"Picked up a drug habit, gambling addiction, and got thrown out of every casino in Vegas?"

Locke snorts. "No. I went backpacking around the world. Saw a lot of Europe."

My eyebrows shoot up in surprise. "No fucking way. That's awesome."

"It was. And when I came home, I felt that accomplishment I was searching for, but—"

"You could have tracked me down whenever you wanted. I couldn't find you. I looked for Sherlock Emerson everywhere. Guess I know why I couldn't find you, *Locke*."

"Things got a little complicated after I got back from Europe. When you and I broke up, it damn near killed me. I'd built up this thing in my head that fate would bring us back together. Whether by chance or … here."

"Ten years …"

He nudges me. "Hey, do you remember one of the first things you ever said to me when I transferred to your school?"

"*You're hot, I'm gay, please tell me you're gay too*? That's my usual line."

Locke laughs. "No. It was, '*My name is Cashton Kingsley. You should remember that because one day it's going to be everywhere.*' You accomplished everything you knew you would when you were sixteen years old. I know I made the right choice back then. Otherwise you wouldn't have all this."

I hate when he's right. Which is always. "What do you do now?" It's weird to me that he's had this whole life I know nothing about.

"I'm one of many financial managers for a casino in Vegas."

"Damn, boy. Guess that's why you're wearing a suit."

"Well, that, and I … I wanted to look good for you." Locke laughs. "It was ironic I spent years trying to forget you only to have you hit it so big there's no escaping you. Or your songs." He leans in. "Your set was amazing by the way. Did you really lose a bet, or was Katy Perry for my benefit?"

"One hundred percent you, and the guys have already told me I owe them. Big-time. I'm kinda picturing foot rubs and guitar tuning for the next year."

"Worth it?"

With the way he's looking at me? "Hell fucking yeah."

"Was …" He licks his lips. "Was the one about the ends of the earth for me too?"

I half want to play on it a bit, but he stares at me with those vulnerable green eyes. "What gave it away? That it was entirely about us or … that it was entirely about us."

Locke smiles.

"Don't be too happy about it. The crowd wasn't too into it. I doubt it'll get recorded."

"Like I care about that. You wrote that song for me. After all these years …"

"You've always been there for me in one way or another. Even if it's only been wistful memories." I lower my head and my voice. "Getting here has basically been my only goal for the last ten years. I'd hoped you'd be here, and even though Seb kept telling me you wouldn't show, I held out. Until Thorne told me you didn't pick up the tickets I left for you. That's why I'm in here at all." I gesture around the bus.

"Seb, huh?" A frown mars his beautiful features. "He's the gay one you grind on every show?"

My insides warm at the pure jealousy oozing from him. "Yep, that'd be the one."

I probably owe him an explanation, but I don't want to give it right now.

He doesn't give anything extra either. "And you thought I stood you up? I bought my own ticket."

"I didn't know what else to think. We haven't seen each other in a *decade*."

"Fair enough." Locke leans back in the seat. "So, let's get the last ten years out of the way and play catch up. Starting with … worst date you've ever had."

I eye him skeptically. "You really want to do this?"

"Why not? If we were mature enough to break up so we could hook up without any guilt, we should be mature enough to talk about it now we're adults."

"You might be an adult. I didn't really mature much after you left."

Locke smiles again, and it's a head trip. The boy I loved is right there. Smiling at me. Looking so damn irresistible and grown-up and put together.

And here I am shirtless. Like I don't even know how to dress myself.

Yeah, that's about right.

"Fine," I relent, "but rules. I only want to hear about your shit dates. No sweet boyfriends or hot, perfect hookups with guys who have bigger dicks than me."

"Wait, that'll mean I can't talk about *any* hookups." The fucker grins.

"Ooh, *burn*. I'd be offended if we both didn't know how untrue that is. You had your hand wrapped around this bad boy not ten minutes ago." I grip my junk. Because I'm a classy act.

"When we started dating in high school, I remember thinking I was bad at giving head because I couldn't fit all of you in my mouth."

I cup his cheek. "Oh, honey, size has nothing to do with that. You *are* bad at giving head."

He swats my hand away. "Fuck you."

"One, you already did. And two, I had to get you back for the dick size joke."

He nods. "Good. For a second there, I thought I was going to have to prove myself."

"Damn it! I take it back. You're terrible, no good, just horrible at sucking dick and need practice."

"Maybe later. I want to know about your life."

"Okay then." I turn and face him. "The important bits. Worst date was a total slimeball who said he was a music producer and had connections. Spoiler: he did not."

"What was his name?"

"Every single guy I met that first year in LA."

Locke laughs.

"Out with it. Your worst date."

"I went out with a guy in Paris, he stuck me with the bill, and then after I paid and we left the restaurant, he pickpocketed me while kissing me goodnight."

I wince. "Ooh, brutal. I was once thrown up on."

Locke's face lights up. "No way."

"And get this, Mr. Vomit is now with another guy I hooked up with who said he doesn't do relationships."

"H-have you had anyone serious since …"

"Nah. This lifestyle isn't conducive for successful relationships." I regret the words as soon as they're out of my mouth. "But, I mean, for the right person—"

He squeezes my hand. "It's okay, I get it. Living and working in Sin City isn't exactly the most innocent. It's probably tenfold on tour."

I shake my head. "I can't believe you ended up back in Nevada after all this time."

"I went to see your mom once."

I pull back. "She never told me."

"Her house was empty. It was in between getting my undergrad and starting my master's."

"Ah. Yeah, she moved out to LA to be closer to me …" I count … "About seven years ago? Now she lives in the house next door to mine."

"That can't be good for your sex life."

I laugh. "I don't bring any guys back to my place."

"I would say that's smart seeing as you're a celebrity and everything, but is it really smart going to theirs? What if they lock you in their basement?"

"Hasn't happened yet, but could you imagine album sales if I got kidnapped?"

Locke frowns. "We may need to reassess your priorities."

Even though it's a joke, I get caught on the "we."

I like the "we." I want us to be a *we* again.

"I think we're all caught up," I whisper. Without hesitation, I press my mouth to his.

Hesitation builds on his lips until he pulls back. "Wait, I

had one more question. It's been driving me crazy for years. It almost made me break my block ban."

I'm intrigued now. "What is it?"

"Cash Me Outside? Really?"

I burst out laughing. "Right? Man, I've had some shitty band names over the years: Cashed Up, Loaded Cash, Cash 22 … but the one to hit it famous is a viral pop culture reference from 2016 hardly anyone remembers."

"I wanted to smack you upside the head."

"Oh, you wanna *cash me outside, how 'bout dat?*"

Locke shakes his head. "You haven't changed a bit, have you?"

"Not at all."

The sadness in Locke's eyes makes me wonder if the same can't be said about him.

CHAPTER SIX
LOCKE

CASHTON IS STILL the boy I fell in love with years ago, despite fame. And I'm … a fucking mess if I truly dissect my life. Taking the only finance job that would have me after having so much time off since getting my MBA, I still feel as lost as I did before I graduated.

I came home from overseas a different person. I was freer, less desperate for professional validation, and the thought of settling down made me edgy. Which wasn't a good sign with a brand-new spouse. I was also dead broke. Student loans, an around-the-world credit card binge, and none of the six-figure jobs I had been offered before still wanted me. Shocking, really, considering I had a degree and no experience after two years.

I had to suck it up and take the only job who wanted me. A business undergrad could do my job.

Yeah, the official title is financial manager, but little fact, casinos in Vegas have so much money going through them, a single casino has countless financial managers checking and double-checking every single dollar.

I don't want to get into it all with Cashton. I don't want to bring this down.

"You know what we should do?" I ask.

"Round two?"

I smile. "Geez, there's the rock star stamina. I need a bit longer. What if we go watch the festival?"

Cashton looks at me skeptically. "You. Want to stand in the desert sun and listen to rock music ..." His eyes narrow. "You're a pod person, aren't you? That's why you've changed your name. That's why you want to do things my Sherlock would've hated."

I roll my eyes. "Ha, ha, *Cashton.*"

"Eww, no. If I have to call you Locke, you have to call me Cash."

That's fair, but ... so weird. Even when he hit fame and the name Cash was everywhere, it was hard to see him as anyone but my Cashton. But I'll do it. For him.

"Come on." I jump up and pull *Cash* up with me. "You can drag me around the place and ramble like you always used to about who's who and fanboy over everyone."

"I'll just put some clothes on." Cash moves toward the back of the bus, past a partition, and then comes out holding a T-shirt. "On a scale of sad to ironic, where does wearing my own band's T-shirt land?"

"Sad scale is a solid three. Ironic scale a nine. But on the narcissistic scale? Like a thirteen."

"I am not narcissistic just because I'm always right ..." He throws the shirt over his head and comes out grinning.

Typical Cash.

"Hey, is it cool if I leave my jacket here? It's hot as balls out, and I feel like an idiot carrying it around." Like I said earlier, I wore the suit so I could look good for him, totally forgetting just how fucking hot the desert is, but it's also an armor of sorts. It makes it look like I have my shit together when I really don't.

Cash looks up at me with dark eyes, the usual gleam of mischief ever present. He pulls my tie from my vest. "You need to get rid of this too. Don't worry, I'll have you looking less businessman and more rock star." He loosens my tie and pulls it through the collar of my shirt.

"Am I not cool enough for you?" I know I'm not cool enough for him. At least that hasn't changed.

He rolls my sleeves up to my elbows. "No one is that cool, but you'll do."

"Tell me that thing again about not being narcissistic."

Cash laughs. He moves to the side of the bus and puts on sunglasses, ties his hair back, and throws a straw hat on his head.

"You look like a cowboy," I point out.

"Yeeha, motherfucker. It's so I won't be recognized. Hopefully."

"Maybe your shirt choice isn't the best, then. What, Mr. Big and Famous can't handle the fans?"

Cash steps forward, leaning up to kiss my lips softly. "I'd rather spend my time listening to you whine about being sunburned than listening to people tell me how awesome I am."

"Shit, you must like me a lot."

Another kiss. "I never stopped."

I never stopped liking him either.

I've been trying to convince myself that what we had in high school was nothing more than young love. That he wouldn't even remember me let alone still like me after all these years.

Yet, here we are, twenty-eight years old, supposedly wiser and more experienced, but I can't help feeling like I'm eighteen again.

Nothing has changed between us, and it's been easy to sink back to where we were. As if no time has passed at all.

The warm desert air hits my face, and Cash is right. It probably won't be long before I'm burning up and complaining about the heat.

Us redheads are like vampires. Pale skin. Don't like direct sunlight. We're basically the same. Minus the bloodsucking thing. Cock-sucking on the other hand …

I side glance at Cash and regret not taking him up on his offer for round two.

"We can stand off to the side behind the barricades," Cash says, leading me toward the mainstage.

The crowd is massive, and it makes sense he wants to hide out instead of trying to blend in out there.

I saw how the people were going crazy for him during his set.

Everyone loves him.

And I know exactly how they feel. He's my Cash amplified when he's in front of a crowd.

He pulls me into a side stage area close to the audience but half-hidden behind equipment and speakers.

It's loud as fuck, not only from the bands but the people's nonstop screaming.

To have twenty thousand people screaming for you, it's surprising Cash is still the same boy I left.

It's impossible to talk, but I don't really need to with Cash. Not having words between us was never a problem. We could sit or stand in comfortable silence probably longer than we should've been able to at seventeen years old.

It's a level of comfort I've never had with anyone else.

Cash moves in front of me, pulling my arms around his waist so I'm holding him from behind.

Ducking my head under the brim of his cowboy hat, I lean in and talk in his ear so he can hear me. "Feels like old times."

We stay like that, watching the band currently on stage who is … I have no idea, but I don't care. Because I have everything I need right here.

"Do you want me to get you something to eat? Or drink?"

I love that he's fussing over me. Like how he bought Dr. Pepper in case I showed up.

"I just need you and what … you apparently call music."

Cash laughs, loud and warm. "You haven't changed at all either."

He's right. In many ways I haven't, but in others …

I've definitely done a lot of stuff I'm not proud of. Things that might make Cash look at me differently. But I also don't want to get into that here.

Cash whistles and cheers for the band as they leave the stage, giving each of the guys a high five or a fist bump, but he never leaves my side.

The one time I try to remove my hand from his hip, he grips on tighter and leaves it there.

Each of the band members eye me, whether out of curiosity or something else, but with Cash holding on to me, I couldn't care less about what anyone else thinks.

While roadies swarm the stage to set up for the next act, I take the opportunity to find out more about Cash and his plans.

"What's your tour schedule like coming up?"

"We actually have a few days off. The boys want to go to Vegas seeing as it's close."

"Vegas, huh? You're gonna be in my part of town?"

"Play your cards right, I'll never leave your ... *part of town.*"

"How do you make everything sound dirty?"

"It's a gift."

Cash looks up at me with the same expression he would in high school when I knew he was about to do something that could get us in trouble.

His chin lifts, moving his mouth closer to mine. He's about to kiss me right here in the middle of this music festival, in front of fans, cameras, and God, and he doesn't even give a shit.

Right before our lips touch, I blurt, "You should do it."

His brow scrunches. "Do what? Kiss you? I was planning on it, and then you had to ruin it by opening your mouth."

"In my defense, I have to open my mouth to kiss you too."

"Stop being a smartass and tell me what you meant."

"You should come back to Vegas with me tonight."

Cash turns in my arms. "Really?"

"It's the last night of the festival, isn't it? Stay with me on your days off, and let's just ... be us again until you have to leave. Cashton and Sherlock."

"Oh, I am so in."

"Yeah?" *We get to get out of this heat?*

"Right after this next set."

So close. "Sounds good. And not at all hot. Or loud. Or crowded."

Cash bursts out laughing. "I'm messing with you. Let's go."

"Oh, thank fuck." I pull him close and smack a big but brief kiss on his lips.

"Come on, you can do better than that." Cash grips my

shirt collar and brings me back in for a deeper kiss that makes my whole body weak.

I moan into his mouth.

Cash's cowboy hat tips backward and falls off his head.

I don't know how much it was working as a disguise, but apparently, it was doing something. The catcalls and Cash's name being called by a group of people on the edge of the barricades breaks us apart.

"Shit. Sorry," he says.

"No sweat. Go say hi."

"We'll be out of here in a sec. I promise."

I watch as Cash makes his way over to the group of fans. He hugs them, takes some selfies while doing the sign of the horns, and even lets two of the girls kiss his cheeks.

He's his natural charismatic self, and they all love it.

I wonder what it would've been like had we tried to make the long-distance thing work. Considering I didn't date the first two years of college, I probably could've pulled it off, but I don't know how I would've handled seeing this kind of stuff on social media—photos of him with people from gigs, looking all happy and having fun.

It's hard enough watching from a few feet away.

I grab his hat that fell on the ground and make my way closer to them just in time to hear them say, "Who's that you're with? Is he famous too?"

I huff. "Nah, I'm no one."

Cash turns to the group. "Actually, he's the inspiration for the song we debuted today."

"The ends of the earth one?" a girl asks.

"That's the one," Cash says easily.

They squee and say how sweet that is, but their high-pitched excitement is drowned out by the awe and shock over Cash acknowledging me in public.

I have no idea what to expect. Cash's orientation isn't a secret in the media. He wasn't one of those celebrities who had to come out in some big interview. The clip that went viral that was his "coming out" was of a paparazzi asking him if it was true he was gay. Cash just laughed as he made his way to his car, surrounded by camera flashes and other questions being thrown at him. But at the last second, he turned to the paparazzo, wore his trademark smirk, and said, "I didn't realize it was a secret." He got in his car and drove off before they could get any follow-up questions out.

I must've watched that clip a million times. It made me feel proud and achy at the same time.

When that happened, it'd been seven years since I'd seen him. Five since I cut him off.

I missed him. I wanted to contact him.

But I couldn't bring myself to do it.

Self-doubt and worthlessness wouldn't let me.

The reason I went to Wharton was because it was what my parents expected of me. I'd already majorly disappointed them by being gay. I figured the least I could do was go into a stable and reputable profession.

Cash was my inspiration to chase a different dream. Granted, it got sidetracked, but the reason I got to explore the world was him.

He finishes with his fans and walks back over to me, cocking his head. "What?"

I place his cowboy hat on his head. "You."

"Me, what?"

Leaning in, I kiss his cheek. "Just you."

I'M sure Locke and I look like a couple of lovesick fucksticks as we walk back to the tour bus. The plan is to grab some stuff for me for a few days and drive off into the sunset in Locke's car.

That plan almost turns to shit when we climb the bus steps and are met by my band. My family, basically. Other than my mom.

Greg and Jasper don't pay much mind. They have groupies hanging off them.

Seb and Thorne, however. They glare daggers at Locke.

"Guy who broke your heart or the one you're going to bury yourself in for days to get over the guy who broke your heart?" Seb asks.

"Wow," Locke says. "They're my options, huh?" He rubs his jaw mockingly. "Can't I be both?"

I snort.

My man can stand on his own and throw down with my friends?

Where has this guy been all my life?

Oh, right. Avoiding me.

I can't say that I'm not upset by that, but I'm definitely on the road to forgiveness. A few more times of being fucked by that amazing cock of his and I'd probably even forgive him for stabbing someone.

Why he'd be stabbing someone, I don't know, but that's not the point.

The point is, I don't care where he's been. I don't care what he's done. All I care about is that he's here with me.

"Everyone, this is Locke Emerson. Locke, this is our manager, Thorne." I point. "My lead guitarist, Seb, drummer, Jasper, and bass player, Greg. The girls are … people I've never met before."

And by the look of Jasper's and Greg's faces, they can't even tell me their names.

Nice.

"Ah," Seb says and stands from his seat at the table. "So, he showed up after all …" He approaches and puffs his chest out in some form of supposed masculinity.

I shove him. "Back down, Seb. No big-brother shit, okay?"

"But I like torturing your boyfriends. It's entertaining when they get all squirmy."

I narrow my gaze because I don't have boyfriends. I have one-night stands. And groupies.

"Boyfriends, huh?" Locke asks with a slight edge in his tone.

"I don't do boyfriends," I say. "I think Seb's messing with you to see how you'll react."

"Okay, fine," Seb says. "I actually meant all those guys I'd scare off by showing up and pretending to be your boyfriend." He laughs. "They'd scramble like I'd lit their farts on fire or something."

"Hmm, how many guys are we talking here?" Locke asks.

I look at my imaginary watch on my wrist. "Oh, wow, look at the time. We should get ready to go if we're gonna hit Vegas before it's too fucking dark to see on these desert roads."

Locke throws his arm around my shoulders. "I'm not under the delusion that you're still the same blushing virgin you were when I met you."

Seb howls with laughter. "This guy popped your cherry? That is so awesome."

"How much did you tell them about our past?" Locke asks.

"Not ... a lot ..."

"Nothing," Seb answers, and I scowl at him.

"He didn't tell us until we booked Death Valley. Then he blurted it all out over a bottle of tequila. That wasn't a fun cleanup."

"Seb. Stop. Talking." I pinch the bridge of my nose.

"You should've seen him on prom night," Locke says. "He—"

I glance up at the roof. "God? If you're up there. Please bring me home now. I'm ready to die of embarrassment. Thanks."

Locke squeezes me close to him. "Oh, honey, you might want to be looking down for that."

"Is this gang up on Cash day?"

"Every day is gang up on Cash day," Locke and Seb say at the exact same time.

Freaky.

Seb smiles. "Okay, I approve. He seems chill enough to deal with your shit." My supposed best friend goes back to his seat.

"That's it?" Locke asks. "That was the extent of my interrogation?"

"Oh, that's just the start," I mumble. "Let me go pack some things and we can head out."

"You're going to Vegas early?" Thorne asks.

"Yup. Locke and I have a lot of catching up to do. Like, a lot."

Thorne looks concerned.

"I mean sex, Thorne. Lots and lots of sex."

"Thanks," Thorne says dryly. "I had no fucking idea what you meant."

Locke's body heat increases to the point I can feel it against me. When I look up at him, his cheeks are pink. I made him blush? It has always been the other way around. This is so awesome.

"What's wrong, then?" I ask Thorne.

"Can you at least let me get a background check on this guy before I let him take you away?"

Beside me, Locke stiffens, but I take hold of his arm and squeeze it in reassurance.

"I've known Locke since I was a kid. He's not a psychopath. So no, you can't do a background check."

The tension leaves Locke's frozen frame.

"Besides, what do I always say when you fear for my life?" I ask.

Thorne sighs. "That you'll be worth more dead than alive."

"Think of the album sales!" I say enthusiastically.

Thorne lets it go, but I don't miss the way he eyes Locke as I pack a bag of clothes and shit I'll need for the next few days.

If Locke notices, he doesn't acknowledge it. He watches me with a warm smile that's so *him*, it makes me move faster.

The sooner we get to Vegas, the sooner our few short naked days together can begin.

I throw my duffel over my shoulder. "See you fuckers in four days outside Caesars."

"You're blowing us off for our whole vacation?" Seb asks.

"Who's gonna come with me to a gay bar seeing as the straight boys over there refuse to?"

Jasper glares. "We only refuse because you always pick up some guy and leave us there without telling us you're going and then laugh the next day when you realize we were hanging out for an hour in a bar with no pussy in sight. None that are interested in *us* anyway."

Seb laughs. "Okay, fair enough, but that is the funnest game ever. Or was until you ruined it by catching on quicker and quicker."

"We're out," I cut in.

I take Locke's hand in my free one but realize as soon as we're off the bus, I have no idea which way to go.

Locke points. "This way."

Walking hand in hand, I'm thrown back to high school and the very first time this ever happened.

Just two inexperienced seventeen-year-olds walking home from school one day because my piece-of-shit car had broken down and Locke had said I could walk him home and then he'd drop me off in his mom's car.

We'd barely gotten a block when he made his move.

Suddenly my hand was in his and my confident exterior I've always been able to show slipped away, revealing an insecure boy who had a serious crush on the new kid in school.

We may be older now, but the feeling is the same.

This guy has me nervous and wanting at the same time. I try to be confident, but my trembling gives away how much he affects me.

"I'm happy you have a team of people who look out for you. It's sweet."

"Yeah, I love to hate them, and they can be annoying as

fuck, but deep down, we all know we've got each other's backs."

"It's good to have that."

"Do you have something like that? I know your mom is pretty absent—"

"How do you know my mom and dad are absent?"

I look down at my feet as they walk over the hardened desert ground. "I might've called once or twice after you blocked me?"

"Oh."

"Yeah. She said you needed to stay away from people like me. And I assume she didn't mean wannabe rock stars." I risk a glance his way.

"You'd be right about that. They didn't take me coming out well at all. It's really only been the last few years they finally let it go, but then …"

"Then what?"

"Well, something happened that made them start again. I've only recently moved back to Nevada, and it hasn't exactly been the warmest welcome."

Locke hasn't told me much about his new life, and I don't know if there's a reason for that or if we just haven't found the right moment yet.

"Then I'll make sure to give you the biggest welcome home."

He nudges me. "It'll be a double celebration. You're finally home too."

Anywhere with you is where I want to make my home.

Yeah, don't say that.

Hello, crazy ex-clinger.

Locke stops walking and tugs on my hand.

I turn to him, pressing our chests together. "What's up?"

"I mean it, Cash. The minute—no, the *second* I saw you again, it was truly like coming home. I've never had that since I was eighteen years old."

I suck in a sharp breath because this is all too much. It's amazing and real and deep, but … it's too much.

Yet, I find myself agreeing with him wholeheartedly. "You're my home too."

&

Locke's hand hits the steering wheel. "Oh fuck, oh fuck, oh fuck."

I laugh around his cock.

"I think we need a rule," he says breathlessly. "No declarations of mushy crap that turns us into horny bastards right before driving so far."

I pull off him and replace my mouth with my hand. "So far. So fucking far."

"Cash …" He throws his head back, but then as if remembering he has to keep his eyes on the road, he grunts and turns his attention back to where we're heading. "If we get run off the road and you die, Thorne will kill me. I assume Seb will too."

"You're the one not wearing a seat belt. If anyone's dying here, it's you."

"*You* took my seat belt off. Right before you attacked me."

"Such a fierce attack too." I pump his cock hard.

"Oh God, oh God, oh God."

"You want this to be over? Give me what I want and the rest of the drive will be a satisfied one."

"What do you want?"

"Your cum in my mouth." I don't give him a chance to respond.

My tongue teases the head of his cock before I take him all the way to the back of my throat. I move my hand to fondle his balls, and the moan he lets out is so loud it drowns out the radio which is on some pop station.

Even his shitty taste in music isn't enough to turn me off him.

Locke thrusts into my mouth. He breathes hard.

And when he comes, I'm too distracted savoring it to freak out about the car taking a massive swerve.

Instead, I pull off him with a laugh. "Wow, you really weren't joking when you said I could run you off the road."

"Your mouth could get us both killed."

"Hmm, dying with your dick out. Both embarrassing and an awesome legacy to leave behind."

"Of course you'd think that. Could you maybe give me a hand here?"

"Geez, I just gave you a blowjob, now you need a handy too?"

"Cash," Locke whines.

"Fine." I reach over and tuck him back in his pants and do up his fly, though from this angle, there's no way I'm getting his button done up. "Good enough."

I feel his stare on me as he continues to drive. "Shouldn't you be paying attention to the road?"

"I should be, but fuck … this is crazy. This whole day has been."

"Yeah, it has." I glance over at him. "And we have the next few days to make it even more memorable."

Locke doesn't miss what I'm insinuating. "If you think I'm going to let you hole up in my hotel room for three days straight, you're going to be disappointed. Let's do Vegas the way we wanted to way back when."

"When we were clearly underage so could never get into anywhere good? Is that what you mean?"

"Exactly. We won't need to use our terrible fake IDs that were so clearly fake."

"I won't need ID at all. I don't know if you know this, but I'm kind of a big deal."

Locke laughs. "As long as you remember you were kind of a big deal to me first, so your fans can't have you."

All I do is smile. It's probably a weird reaction to have.

We do a lot for our fans. Our private lives are splashed over the media like it's entertainment. We've accepted it and know it's part of the lifestyle we lead.

Deep down, I hate the celebrity title. I love being famous, but I still feel like *me*. Not some over-the-top celebrity. And Locke claiming me and wanting me to be all his and not belong to my fans, it makes me want this for real.

I want to be Locke's again.

I want to find a way to make it work.

But unless a casino on the Strip suddenly wants to book Cash Me Outside as a Vegas residency act, I don't see how it could work when I'm constantly on the road. After this tour, we'll be back in LA recording another album, but maybe I could convince the guys to do a writing retreat somewhere out here in the desert.

Though, I don't know how much writing I'd get done if Locke was in the same vicinity as me.

"What're you thinking about?" Locke asks.

"How to turn three days into three months."

Locke hums. "That would be nice."

"Okay, let's shake off thoughts of the inevitable. You

should tell me what we're gonna do in Vegas and where you're going to take me."

"There's a hot new gay bar open in my casino."

"Your casino, huh?"

"Well, my boss's casino. Where I live. But yeah, same thing, right?"

"Why do you live in a hotel?"

Locke side-eyes me. "It's a long story."

"Well, how long have we got until we're there?"

He looks like he contemplates giving up the full details, but then he changes his mind. "I'd rather hear about your life as a rock star. Is it everything you thought it would be?"

"It's everything and more. It's hard work. It can be crazy. But ... I fucking love it."

"You were born to do it."

"Just like you were born to work with numbers in that genius brain of yours."

Locke purses his lips. "Maybe."

"Maybe?"

"You know why I took off for Europe as soon as I had my master's?"

"Because you spent seven years studying without a break and deserved a vacation?"

"I realized I'd spent all that time and energy getting a degree I didn't even want. I did it for my parents, not for me. I did it because I thought numbers came easy, so it was the right choice. But ..."

"You hate it?"

"It's so boring."

I laugh. "Duh, I told you that all through senior year when you were studying for all your advanced math classes that confused the shit out of me. The alphabet does not belong in math."

"It does belong in math, but let's not get into this decade-old argument."

"How about you tell me what you do want to do with your life, then?"

"Is becoming Cash Me Outside's groupie a real job?" Locke asks. "Because I'd take that in a heartbeat."

"Say the word and I'll create a position for you on my team somewhere. Anywhere. I don't care."

His eyes go back to the road. "As nice as that fantasy is, I've only been at this new job a few months. I don't want to fuck that up."

"But if you've only been there a few months, you're not exactly committed. They wouldn't be holding you to any long promises you've made."

"It's … complicated. My boss has done a lot for me without really knowing me. I don't want to let him down."

"Like you didn't want to let your parents down, so you went to school and studied something you don't even like?"

"Touché."

"Okay, real talk."

"As opposed to the fake talk we've been doing this whole time?"

"Don't snark at me, nerd."

"Don't call me a nerd. I mean … can you really still call me that?" Locke gestures to his filled-out body.

"Are you still all smart and genius-like? Your nerdiness had nothing to do with your scrawny ass. I loved your scrawny ass."

"I wasn't scrawny," he mumbles. "I was lanky."

"Okay, well, what does your lanky ass want to be when he grows up? Real talk now."

He sighs. "You know, I was hoping all the travel would help me figure it out, but I guess I don't have that thing."

"I hope you have a thing, but I take it you're not using it as a euphemism for a dick, because unless my mouth is mistaken, it was just wrapped around your *thing*."

"For real, Cash. You have music. You've always loved music. It's been music or bust for you for as long as I've known you. I've never been that passionate about anything. Except maybe …" Locke bites his lip. "Except maybe you."

"If you remember correctly, I was willing to give up LA for you, so you have to be pretty fucking special. And that means you're special enough to find what you love doing. Whatever it is, you should go for it. And, if it's something like be a luggage bitch for a rock band, I know some people."

Locke laughs. "Thanks. I'll keep that in mind."

"Thorne might need an assistant. He complains about having to kick groupies out of hotel rooms the morning after. Says it makes him feel like a pimp and isn't in his job description."

"You guys actually make him do that?"

"Well, not so much anymore. He got smart and started coming in earlier and earlier. Seb finally said enough when Thorne interrupted mid-blowjob and said it was time to go."

"Poor Seb."

"In all seriousness, though. Whatever you choose to do, I know you'd rock it. Unless it was singing. Because, you know I love you, but your voice …" I screw up my face. "Not really a serenading kind of screech."

Instead of laughing like I thought he would, Locke's eyes bore into me. The intensity hits me with such force it takes a moment to realize I said I love him. Not *loved* him. But love him. Right now. And it fell out of my mouth so easily, like a reflex. Like muscle memory took over.

It was like it really was ten years ago and we were driving home from Death Valley after attending as patrons instead of me being a headliner.

Slipping into our old ways is as natural as my draw to him has always been.

As much as that is a good thing, it's also fucking scary.

It puts pressure on these next few days, and I don't know if I'll be able to recover.

Being with Locke again might damn near kill me.

CHAPTER EIGHT
LOCKE

NERVES HIT me as I pull into the parking garage behind the Catalina Resort and Casino.

I'm nervous about letting Cash into my life and him seeing … someone who's not me. Or, not the boy he remembers.

My apartment is a small suite. It has hotel furnishings and no real touches of my personality.

And as soon as we step through the door, he notices it. I can tell.

"It's only temporary," I say.

"You haven't been here long?"

I shake my head.

"What happened to your last place?"

I try to force the words to come out. *My last place was my spouse's. Ex-spouse. Because I was married.*

Even though marrying Shannon was a mistake and we're in the very last stages of the divorce proceedings, the thought of Cash standing at an altar and promising his life to someone else hurts my heart so hard, I don't want to do that to him.

"It's complicated."

Cash and I have four days together. After that ... I've got no idea. We need to live in the moment. Take this opportunity as a gift instead of what it is—a recipe for heartbreak.

"What do you want to do first?" I ask.

"Shower. Then hit the slots."

"What you call me?" I exclaim.

"Come shower with me and I might repeat it." The heat in Cash's eyes never fails to get me going.

The image of me on my knees in the shower and proving my deep-throating skills flashes through my mind, and there's no way I won't be doing that.

"Fine. Shower. But we're not spending the whole four days in this room having sex."

"Hmm, we'll see." Cash starts undressing on his way to the bathroom, and damn it, we're so going to be spending the next four days fucking.

It takes Cash no time at all to come down my throat. I remember everything that used to do it for him, remember the way he tastes, but most of all, I remember the look of awe in his eyes when he'd stare down at me, watching as his cock disappeared between my lips.

None of it has changed.

When we do finally manage to drag our asses out of the shower, he dresses in dark jeans and a plain black tee and throws on his leather jacket, while I don my black dress pants and a button-down.

"I feel overdressed," I say.

"You look overdressed. I suggest taking off the pants and shirt."

"Not what I mean, and you know it."

"You look hot enough to fuck," Cash says. "Wanna stay in and do that instead?"

I laugh. "You will not win this. We're Vegas'ing it up, baby."

"If you insist, but I have a way we can make it go by superfast."

"Yeah?"

"We set a limit we're allowed to spend on each game. So, like, we can only put five hundred into the slots. A grand at any of the tables. Once we lose, we move on."

My mouth might be hanging open right now. "Sure, but you might want to reduce those bets to say fifty and a hundred bucks?"

"Ooh, you're right. The less money, the quicker we do everything so we can come back here and fuck."

"I meant because that's more in my budget, but that aside, you literally came ten minutes ago. Do you really need to go again?"

Cash steps closer to me and presses his impressive chest against mine. "I only have you for four days. I'm going to come as many times as I can."

"That sounds like a challenge."

"Challenge accepted. Now, let's go get this over with." He plants a quick kiss to my lips and then grabs my collar and drags me out of my room.

Despite saying he's going to rush it, we take our time making our way through the casino next to the Catalina. As an employee, I'm not allowed to gamble at my own casino.

We play blackjack, lose some money in the slots, and play a few rounds of roulette. There's only one game we lose in five seconds flat.

"Okay, so craps is … crappy. Moving on." Cash walks off.

I laugh.

No one has recognized him yet, which I'm thankful for. A

few have done a double take, but considering he doesn't have a huge entourage, isn't in any VIP or high-rollers' rooms, I assume people think he's a lookalike or an impersonator, or maybe they can't place him without the rest of the band.

He's definitely famous, but not so famous he can't walk down the street without being stopped.

"Poker tables?" he asks.

That's cute. "You do know a game of poker takes hours, right?"

Cash screws up his face. "That's out. Didn't you say something about a gay bar?" He steps closer to me. "I'm ready to grind on a dance floor until you're so hard you'll take me back to your room and we won't leave for four days."

I take his hand. "This way."

There's an exit that leads to the walkway back across the street to the Catalina.

Cash wastes no time trying to pull me straight to the dance floor, but I tug on his hand.

"Drink?" I yell over the music.

He hesitates.

"We're supposed to be doing Vegas right."

"We can have a couple and dance them off. I don't want us to be drunk when I do *you* right." He's ridiculous but so utterly Cash.

I crook my finger at him to come closer, and I capture his mouth with mine.

The beat of the music thrums around us, people ignore us as they bump by, but I keep kissing my teenage dream and memorize this fleeting moment while holding on for as long as I can.

One shot turns into two. Two turns into four. And then Mr. Sober Rock Star drags a tipsy me out onto the dance floor.

I sway.

"Dude, you can't be drunk already. You used to be a bartender."

"Like, two years ago. I haven't drunk much since."

"I'll just have to pull you close and hold you up, my little lightweight."

"Oh no, how horrible for me!" I'm not that drunk, but that won't stop me from leaning into him.

We're in our own little Cashton and Sherlock bubble, and I never want to leave it.

But that's not reality. That's not *our* reality.

My reality catches my eye. Shannon stands by the side of the dance floor with a wide smile on their face.

Ah, shit.

They take a step toward me, and I freeze. I'm not ready for them to meet. I'm not ready to tell Cash the truth.

I lean in next to Cash's ear. "I'll be right back. Gotta take care of something."

He looks up at me all glassy-eyed and happy. "Okay."

Before I can walk away, Cash touches his lips to mine. It's awkward and weird, but only because I'm letting it be.

Shannon and I are one hundred percent over, and even though I've seen Shannon with other people since we split and I'm okay with it, I feel weird flaunting something in front of them when it was ultimately my lack of interest in being in the marriage that was our downfall.

I pull away. "Back soon."

I know he's watching me as I walk away, but I'm going to make this quick.

"Hey." I take Shannon's arm and lead them away from the dance floor.

"What, I don't even get to meet him? Ripped off."

"Not … now." Or ever.

"Oh. You haven't told him about us."

"We have four days together, Shan. That's it. I'm not going to bring the mood down."

A concern line forms above their brow.

"It's fine. Is there really a perfect time to go into the whole divorce thing on a date?"

"Well, preferably before you have sex with them."

My face falls.

"Holy shit, really? Go you." They playfully shove me.

"We have ten years to catch up on and a limited time to do it. I don't think introducing him to my ex will really let us have the best time together."

They look disappointed, but they understand. "Just promise to introduce me one day."

I huff a laugh. "Sure. Because, you know, I'm going to see him again after this week and everything."

"Why not?"

"He's a famous rock star. He tours the world, and I …" *I'm just a numbers guy.*

"You're a wanderer too. Don't tell me that you're not. If we didn't have to move back because of our visas, you know you'd still be over there slinging beers and making your way through countries and continents being free."

I never realized that's how Shannon saw me.

Shannon steps forward. "Please don't rule out a future with him. You basically did that with us the minute we got back from venturing the world, and look where it got you. I love you, and I always will, but we both deserved better. Don't let anything get in the way of what you want."

They don't understand.

They may understand me, but Cash's life … it's not something you can just tag along for the ride. It's not a normal life.

I scoff. Then again, the idea of a "normal life" is what made me run off to Europe to begin with.

"I should get back to him."

Shannon nods, but I feel their judging stare all the way back.

Some small dude is trying to dance with Cash, but my man is standing there oblivious. His focus is only on me.

And when I get close, he pushes past the other guy.

Then his mouth is on mine, hot and demanding, and I'm so not complaining.

"Who was that?" he asks when he finally pulls back.

"Wha? I can't even remember my name after that kiss."

He stares up at me with heat in his eyes. "Ready to call it a night?"

Something Shannon said about telling Cash the truth before I sleep with him pings in my brain, and while that ship sailed two orgasms ago, maybe they have a point.

"How about we drink some more?" I ask.

I expect him to protest, but he doesn't.

Maybe Cash can sense the shift in me since running into Shannon, or maybe I'm reading into it.

So, we drink.

A lot.

Damn, this guy can put them away.

I mean, it makes sense. He's a rock star.

Still. How has he not ended up with alcohol poisoning at some point in the last ten years?

He chuckles when he sees how glassy-eyed I am. "You're *soooo* drunk."

I smile. "You don't sound so sober yourslef."

"Your*slef*, hey?" Cash's hand runs down my chest. "You're so hot. You always were."

I'm pretty sure he's the only person who found my lanky, fair-skinned, and freckled body hot in high school, but I don't care about that. I've only ever cared that he saw me that way.

"Let's go dance again," I say, but when I try to stand, my legs don't seem to work anymore. "Shit." I grab the edge of the bar to hold myself up, but it doesn't work too well.

Arms come around me, and I lock eyes with my savior.

Cash laughs. "And you're so adorable when you're drunk."

"It's so unfair," I whine.

"What is?" Cash asks.

"Timing. Courage … Life."

"And I think it's time we get you out of here."

"'Kay."

But instead of leading me to the elevators to go upstairs, Cash leads me outside the club and casino and onto the street.

Cash pushes me against the side of the building so he's not the only one holding me up.

I lean back, resting my head against the brick.

The millions of people on the street don't pay mind to us. This is Vegas. There are more drunk people than sober.

I laugh. "You're a bad influence. I can't keep up."

"Dude, the guys in my band can't keep up." He rubs his stomach. "Although, it's sitting weird in my gut. It probably got used to the break I had, and now it doesn't know what the fuck is going on."

Once I get some fresh air—er, some *Vegas air*—into me, I feel more stable and a little less emo.

"Get wasted at a bar. We can check that off what we wanted to do way back when."

Cash laughs. "Guess so." He shoves his hands in his tight pockets. "You want to tell me who that … person was?"

I cock my head. "How'd you know they were enby?"

"I didn't. But by the look of them, I didn't want to assume gender."

"They usually get 'What are you?' Pisses them off. People have no tact."

"You're not answering the question."

I let out the loudest sigh known to man. "Because I don't want to."

"They're an ex, I'm guessing?"

I rub my chest. "This will change everything."

He stumbles back. "Oh God, are you still together? Was this, like, some fucked-up famous hall pass or something?"

Cash looks absolutely horrified, and it breaks my heart he could think that of me.

"No." I lunge for him. And miss. Because my balance is all skewed. I manage to grab his wrist. "I swear, it's not that. We're not together. Not anymore."

He sags in relief.

"But … we are still married."

Cash pulls out of my grasp. "You're fucking married?"

"Separated. Divorce papers are signed and everything. It just hasn't been finalized because we got married in the Netherlands, not here, and there was a lot of red tape."

I have no idea if my words are coming out right. I have a feeling they're a slurred mess.

"Cashton, please …"

He stares at me with hurt in his eyes. "You got married. *Married!*"

"It was a mistake. The biggest. We both knew that really early on."

"That doesn't change the fact you stood in front of a minister and promised your life to someone else. That you could possibly be that much in love when ..." He shakes his head.

"I told you things got complicated," I say quietly.

He folds his arms. "Then uncomplicate it. Do you love them?"

"I don't know how to explain Shannon. They ... they were there for me when I was lost, and I mistook that for something that it wasn't. I needed someone—"

"You should've come to *me*."

"I *couldn't!*" I hang my head.

"I haven't so much as had a relationship since you. I've barely even tried because it has never felt right. Definitely not enough to stand at an altar declaring eternal love. So am I the moron here? What is this?" He waves a hand between us. "A fling with some guy from high school who didn't mean shit? A fuck down memory lane? Screw you, *Sherlock.*"

"It's not like that. When I met Shannon, I needed ... *something.* I just didn't know what. You had your fame and your rock star life. You had everything, and I—"

"I didn't have *you*! It turns out I *never* stopped loving you, but you can't say the same."

I don't know what to say. "I ..."

"Cash Kingsley!" a voice screams from our right.

"Cash!" Another one.

Paparazzi.

Shit.

"Go back upstairs," he mutters to me.

"Cashton ..." I whine.

"Just go. I'm gonna head to Caesars and find the guys. Tell

them the media knows we're in Vegas." He turns to the cameras. "Hey." He smiles and waves politely.

"What are you doing in Vegas?" a photographer asks.

"Who's that with you?"

Cash steps in front of me. "Just a fan. Take your photos and move on, guys. Surely, I'm not the most famous person here tonight."

Just a fan.

A few hours ago, I was the guy he wrote his latest song for. Now I'm just a fan.

Got it.

I turn on my heel and stumble my way back inside the casino.

CHAPTER NINE
CASH

I USE the key card the front desk gave me to let myself into Seb's room. Being famous is good like that. I got the key, no questions asked.

The guy on his knees giving Seb a blowjob isn't even a shock to me anymore. Seen it all before.

"Get out," I say.

Seb's eyes fly open. "Cash, what the fu—"

The twink pulls off Seb's cock with a loud slurp. "Cash Kingsley?" He gasps. "Oh my God, this is so awesome! Are you going to join us?" He stands, completely naked, his cock long and thin, and I'm not even remotely interested.

I give my best friend *the look*.

"Sorry, babe. Band business." Seb pulls up his pants and hands his trick his clothes.

"How long are you in Vegas for?" The poor guy has hope in his eyes.

"I'll call you." Seb pushes a now dressed rando toward the door.

"You don't have my number."

"Our manager is, like, FBI agent level of smart when it comes to getting intel. He'll find you."

"Oh. You want my name?"

"I'll guess it."

I snort and then cover my mouth. Seb sure knows how to make me feel better even when he's not trying to.

He closes the door and leans against it, letting out a loud breath. "I don't know whether to thank you or hate you right now. His mouth was amazing, but he had stage five clinger red flags. Your heartbreak couldn't have waited ten more minutes before I got a chance to blow my load?"

I frown. "How'd you know it was heartbreak?"

"Because you left us in the desert a few hours ago all happy and loved up. You've had exactly enough time for three rounds of fucking, and that's the top end of your attention span when it comes to dating."

I flop down on his bed. Then I think better of it. I sit up. "What round were you on?"

Seb laughs. "You're safe. You interrupted the opening act."

I lie back down. "Locke's married."

"He's *what*?" Seb turns to leave. "Where is he? I'll kill him." He gets as far as opening the door.

"He's *separated*," I call out. "Technically."

Seb calms down almost immediately. "Oh. And you're being a little bitch about that, why?"

"Because he moved on." My voice is all mumbly and depressed.

Seb moves to lie on the bed next to me. "I don't understand. Have you been lying about hooking up with all those guys on tour?"

"That was just sex. I don't give a shit how many guys

Locke has fucked. I mean, I don't want to hear about it, but that's not why I freaked out. He fell in *love*. He promised to have and to hold until death do they part. That's … Grrargh."

"But it didn't work out. So, it was actually promise to have and to hold until we realize we made a mistake."

"No, no, no, no, no. We aren't doing this. You can't be on his side and use logic. He's divorced … or almost divorced, but that doesn't negate that he was once in the headspace that he'd found his forever in a superhot enby god…ess. Shit, what's the nonbinary word for god?" I click my fingers. "Deity. They're a fucking deity."

"What are you rambling about?"

I groan. "His ex is beautiful."

Seb rolls onto his side. "Are you serious right now?"

"What?"

He nudges me. "You are *Cash Kingsley*, and you're intimidated by his non-famous ex? You don't get intimidated. Ever."

Seb's right. I don't.

"They got a piece of Locke I'll never have, and I hate them for it. And I hate Locke for moving on. And I hate …" I suck in a sharp breath. "I hate I spent the last ten years without him."

"Makes total sense why you're in *my* bed instead of being with him right now making up for lost time."

God, I hate Seb makes a point.

"The thing I'm realizing is I've always seen myself as *his*. He was the one that got away. My regret. My heart locked on him, and it never let go. Those feelings might have been buried over the years, but there's no denying we belong together. I don't care if it's been less than a day since we met again. It was there the minute we saw each other—that spark. That forever feeling I've never experienced with anyone else."

Seb shifts and rolls away from me, reaching for the bedside

table for some hotel stationery. He throws a pen and paper on my stomach. "Write that shit down, man. There's our next hit."

"I don't want to write. I just want to wallow."

"You're an idiot."

"*You* are."

"Mature."

I shove him.

"Fine, if you're not going to take advantage of your stupidity, I will." He takes the notepad and starts writing shit down.

"Thank you for exploiting my heartache."

"Ooh, good line."

"Fuck, I hate you."

Seb pats my head. "Sleep off your anger and go talk to him tomorrow when you're less … emo."

I flip him off, but he's right. Maybe I need to sleep on it.

It's unfair of me to be mad Locke moved on when we've had no contact for eight years. Widowers remarry faster than that. But I guess the difference is there's no chance of their lovers coming back.

Maybe meeting up with Locke again was stupid.

I might not have had any successful relationships in the last ten years, but I've been mostly happy.

Hearing him say he was married was like saying goodbye to him all over again. He hollowed out my heart, taking the important part with him.

Faith in us dimmed to a level I never experienced even as a teenager.

I don't want to lose him this time, but maybe I already have.

Maybe I'm the only one with this intense draw, and he's in his room right now thinking I'm totally overreacting.

Okay, and I probably am.

I totally am.

I sigh.

Seb climbs off the bed and grabs his acoustic guitar. He plays with melody and lyrics, while I listen to my stupid emotions being put on display.

The song is raw and painful.

I rub at the dull ache in my chest.

Seb's voice lulls me into sleep, where I dream of a life filled with regret and loneliness.

It's a familiar feeling, and only one man has ever made me experience it.

I don't want to go through that again.

$$\oint$$

My eyes fly open, and I sit up. "What time is it?"

Seb's asleep next to me, and light streams into the hotel room through the tiny gap in the curtains.

He mumbles something that sounds like "fuck off" and rolls over.

I search for my phone but can't find it, so I climb over Seb and take his.

He opens his eyes and grumbles. "I got excited until I realized it was you on top of me."

"Love you too." His phone says it's 10:00 a.m. "Shit." I jump out of bed.

I have to make this right. God, Locke probably hates me. I wouldn't blame him.

"Come to the conclusion you're being a dick and need to go apologize yet?" Seb yawns.

"I hate that you know me so well." I head for the bathroom.

"Trust me, so do I," Seb calls after me.

I spin on my heel to face him. "Did you finish the song?"

"Yep."

"Come teach it to me while I shower. We're gonna need it for all the groveling."

"Maybe we should have a talk about boundaries."

I wave him off. "You've seen my dick a billion times. I saw yours just last night."

"And what do you think Locke will think about us seeing each other naked and sharing a bed? You were freaking out about him marrying someone else, but I have some sad news for you: you and I are practically a married couple. Minus the sex."

"We are not," I say but suddenly gain new perspective.

I love Seb. I really do. Two days ago, if he'd got down on one knee and asked me to marry him, I probably would've shrugged and gone with it. Not because I'm *in love* with him. But because he's comfortable. He's a permanent fixture in my life. Marrying him is a smart move for me professionally. There'd be a million reasons why marrying him would work. And inevitably not work. Because getting married for any reason other than true love won't last. Companionship doesn't equal fairy-tale love. It helps, but it's not the type that makes your stomach flutter and your toes curl.

"Holy shit, we're totally an old married couple."

And I need to grovel more than I thought.

I was expecting to need to forgive him, but the truth is he never did anything wrong.

I'm the one who needs to be full of apologies.

"Sorry," Seb says as if the revelation is somewhat disappointing.

"Don't be. You gave me the best gift I could've been given."

"A husband who cheats on you repeatedly?"

I laugh. "Perspective. I need to kiss Locke's feet and worship the ground he walks on."

Seb smiles. "Then let's teach you your groveling song."

Under the warm spray and the harsh lighting in the hotel bathroom, I regret everything about how that went down.

Seb plays for me while I scrub up, and he really did do an amazing job making my wallowing sound less whiny and more angsty.

I'm ashamed at the way I acted toward Locke and need to make it up to him.

I bang my head on the shower wall and then remember I'm in Vegas and that could be hazardous to my health. There could be anything in this room, and I'm not too eager to get a blacklight and find out what.

But I probably deserve it. I need to get over myself if I want anything to do with Locke ever again.

My Sherlock.

We both grew up, him more than me, but that was always going to happen.

We've lived our separate lives, and we've seen the world. He's discovered another love. Experienced heartache again. But for me, there was no recovering after him.

I have no doubt walking away when we were eighteen years old was the wrong decision, but how were we to know no one else would fill our hearts the way we each did back then?

Life experiences.

Love.

Lust.

Sex.

We needed to do all of that to get here.

We left it up to fate to meet again, and now's our time.

I shut off the water and dry off, racking my brain about how I can fix this.

A song won't be enough. At least, not for me.

I need to make him fall in love with me again.

"I'M SORRY, sir. I can't give out personal information about any guests staying here let alone a celebrity." The hotel clerk stares like she's better than me, and I'm about to lose my shit.

After only a couple hours of broken sleep thanks to being drunk for the first time in forever and wanting the room to stop spinning, I knew I had to try to find Cash.

I need to explain while I'm sober and lucid.

I need him to understand why I married Shannon and why it was the second biggest mistake of my life.

The first was going to Wharton instead of following Cash to LA and going to college in California.

I want to put the regrets of the last ten years behind us and start again even if I don't know how that will work with a rock star and a no one.

"Look, I know you can't tell me what room Cash is in, but can you call his room and tell him I'm in the lobby waiting for him? Please?"

The clerk is getting as frustrated with me as I am with her, but she gives me a smile through gritted teeth. "Even if Cash

Kingsley was a guest, I wouldn't do that, but he's not registered here anyway, so you're wasting your breath."

"He's famous. He's probably checked in under an alias."

"The rest of the band is. Mr. Kingsley is not."

Finally getting somewhere. "Seb. The bass player. He knows me. I'm not some stalker fan, for fuck's sake." I take my hotel ID out even if this isn't an affiliate to the one I work at. "I'm an employee at the Catalina. I was with Cash last night, and I need to see him."

She scoffs. "Yeah, okay. I spent my night with a Hemsworth brother."

I barely resist banging my pounding head on the desk in front of me.

I'm hungover, unshowered, I'm still in my clothes from last night, my jaw is scruffy, and I probably look like a homeless person. I can't hate her for not trusting me, but why can't she, damn it? I could really do with some old-fashioned benefit of the doubt type crap.

"Sherlock Emerson!"

I still at the name. The name only one person would use other than my parents, and that deep, raspy voice is definitely not from them.

The voice is far away but still in this room.

The desk clerk's mouth drops open, and I don't even get the chance to give her a smug look because I spin so fast, I almost fall over.

There Cash stands, across the foyer near the elevator banks, looking a hell of a lot less messy than me.

Seb stands with him, pulling a guitar out of his case while Cash says something to him without taking his eyes off me.

My feet move closer to him but stall when he starts singing.

Forever was separated by distance
Thousands of miles
A decade of regrets
We tried living apart
But you're locked in my heart

I blink and glance around the stanky-ass Vegas casino, wondering if I'm still drunk.

But no, this is definitely happening.

People crowd around us, creating a circle, and taking out their phones.

I suck in a sharp breath as Cash continues to sing about us.

The song about us he sang at Death Valley was cute and romantic. This … this is raw and emotional. It hurts because the truth is painful. But it *is* the truth.

He's in my heart. He always has been. Always will be.

Seb continues to play, and Cash sings as they take steps toward me.

They keep coming, but I'm frozen to the spot.

You're locked in my heart.
You're locked in my heart.

The more he sings those words, the more I understand. I hurt him when I married Shannon, but as painful as it is, he knows we belong together.

He finishes the song, but I'm still frozen.

I can't move.

I want to reach for him and beg and plead, but I want to kiss him more.

My feet take the smallest steps toward him. I cup the back of his head, my hand threading through his long hair. "Cash …"

He nods. "It's okay. I know."

"You know what?"

"That you love me."

"Always have," I admit.

"Always will."

His lips touch mine, so strong and sure. And I have no doubt that if we try, we can make us work.

I don't know the logistics right now, and I don't really care so long as I'm with Cash.

I'm willing to do what I wasn't able to ten years ago.

Even though cameras and people are all watching this play out, I don't hold back.

I slip my tongue into his mouth and pour my heart and soul into every nip. Every lick. Every taste.

When he rests his forehead against mine and breaks the kiss, I breathe him in.

"I want to be with you," he murmurs. "I know that might seem impossible right now, and—"

"I'll follow you anywhere you go."

He pulls back, his deep brown eyes wide. "You will?"

"The only time over the last ten years I have felt like myself was when I was traveling. But I still had a missing piece. *You.*"

Cash attacks my mouth again, this time even more forceful.

I feel it in the way he kisses me.

His promise of forever.

The thing that's been holding me back for a decade is the same thing that will set me free.

Cash and I will never change.

It'll be me and him always.

"We should probably go somewhere and talk," I say against his mouth.

"No. Take me back to your room. We have forever to talk."

The analytical side of me wants to sit us down and hash this out, but when the word "forever" falls from his lips, I believe him.

We'll have tomorrow to talk through how we can make it work.

We'll have the next few days to make future plans.

And we'll have forever to love each other.

Right now, I'm going to take his hand and lead him back to my place, lay us down, and offer him everything I have.

I'm going to give him all of me, no holding back.

We push our way through the growing crowd, and Seb helps with keeping fans back.

There are cheers and applause from the audience that has gathered, some of them not entirely sober from last night.

Cash's name is called out from every direction.

I've seen it happen in paparazzi videos and on TMZ, but being beside him as it happens is surreal.

This is the type of crazy I'm going to have to get used to.

And I'm here for it.

I wouldn't change it for the world because it's exactly what Cash set out to do. If he lets me be in his world at all, I'm the luckiest man that has ever lived.

In the bright morning of Vegas, the seediness of the city can't even bring me down.

It's a race back to my hotel room, and thankfully, we lose the crowd somewhere around the Bellagio.

By the time we get back to my room, it's just Cash and me, our heavy breathing and wandering hands.

I'm dying to kiss him again, but I know if I start, I'm not going to be able to stop.

Once his mouth is on me, I'll want it on me for the next few hours.

This isn't going to be a quick fuck.

Even if I'm dying for everything here and now, I need to show him how patient I can be.

I'll be patient while he's on the road.

I'll wait for him stage side while he's on tour.

I'll be there for him, no matter what. No matter where.

I'm his.

I'll always be his.

While kicking the door closed behind me, I reach for his shirt.

Cash leans in for that kiss I'm so desperate to give him but can't. Not yet.

I cover his mouth with my hand so I'm not tempted. "Lose our clothes first."

He mutters against my palm, but it comes out as a muffled mess.

"What?" I drop my fingers to his fly.

"I said you're so impatient."

"On the contrary. Once I have you naked, I'm going to have the patience of a saint.

You'll get my mouth, and you'll get my lips. My tongue. I'm going to taste every inch of you. I'll lick you until you can't take it anymore, and you won't hold back while you tackle me and bury your cock inside my ass and lose yourself in me."

"Fuck, Locke … You're gonna let me in here?" He grips my ass and pulls me against him.

"Whenever you want," I whisper.

Our mouths are back to being so close, inches apart, but we've made no progress on the clothing front.

I can tell he's going to test me this whole time, and I'm looking forward to it.

"Get naked and land your bare ass on the couch, while I get supplies," I order. I don't need to watch to know he'll do it.

I go to my room and try to remember where I put all my sex stuff since moving in. I've had a *huge* need for it. Obviously. With my lonely, celibate self.

In a box under my bed, I find everything I need. I grab the lube and condoms, but I pause on the vibrating plug I have in there.

I wonder if the batteries will still work considering it's been so long since I've used it.

The thought of prepping myself for Cash so he can just slide inside me has me reaching for it.

I test it, and the loud buzzing has my ass yearning to feel it inside me.

"Sherlock," Cash calls out, and I jump. "Hurry up."

"Stop being so impatient!"

"If you're not back out here in ten seconds, I'm gonna take things into my own hands."

"Don't you dare touch yourself. Sit on your hands and stop being a demanding diva."

A half moan, half growl floats in from the other room, making me laugh. I love how after all these years, he'll still do as I say.

As quickly but carefully as I can, I lube up the toy and slowly work myself open with it until it won't slip out of me as soon as I let it go.

It takes a few minutes to get there, so by the time I do make my way back out to the living area, Cash is sitting on his hands and looking miserable. His long hair hangs down his naked shoulders.

He's gotten only hotter in the last ten years, and I have no doubt that every time I see him naked for the foreseeable future, I'm going to be taken aback by his striking features. His hard jaw, warm brown eyes …

"Fucking finally. What took you so—" He must see the way I'm walking a bit funny. "Whatcha got back there?"

I turn and wiggle my butt at him, the thick base of the plug sticking out.

"All is forgiven. Get that ass over here."

"Not yet." I step toward him and hand him the remote for the toy. "I have plans for you. Anytime you get too close to the edge, hit the button."

He shifts in his seat. "This is going to be fun."

"Or torture." *For both of us.* "But think how good it will be when you're finally allowed to let go." I sink to my knees.

His cock stands tall and hard, while his skin looks sticky with precum.

"Aww, baby. Did you get a little excited?"

"Fuck you. You told me I couldn't touch myself, and apparently my dick likes that."

"A lot." I lean in and lick up the sticky substance off his lower stomach.

His wet cock hits me in the chin, and I move my mouth there next.

Cash's whole body tenses as he lets out a loud "Fuck" while my tongue glides over the head of his dick.

I swallow him down, tasting more of that salty precum.

The long moan that comes out of Cash's mouth is accompanied by a sudden vibrating in my ass.

I pull back fast before I clamp down on his dick. "Oh, shit," I breathe.

"Now that's a handy trick," Cash says, but I'm too busy riding out the sensation pressing against my prostate.

I lay my head on Cash's thigh, trying to catch my breath.

His free hand threads through my short hair while he clicks the remote again to turn it off.

"This is definitely going to be torture," I say.

"That's what love with me is like. I'm gonna make it hurt so good."

"Wow, rip off Jon Mellencamp much? He'll sue you, you know."

Cash snorts. "I don't think he was singing about sex acts."

"I totally think he was."

He goes to argue, but I turn my head and lick my way along the underside of his hard cock. That shuts him up real fast.

"Nngh, that mouth."

"Mmm, your dick." I take him all the way in my mouth again.

He squirms as his hard cock slides in and out between my lips. It's as if he's trying to tell me to stop, it's too much, but his hips are only inviting more as they thrust up.

Cash grunts every time the head of his dick hits the back of my throat, and when I glance up at him through my lashes, our eyes lock.

"Shit, shit, fuck … stop." He fumbles with the button again, hitting it just in time for me to pull off his dick.

My hands grip his thighs, my nails digging into his skin while I try not to come. The vibration gets me close to the edge in no time, but I refuse to blow my load this fast. I want Cash inside me when that happens.

So we keep playing this game. When I'm not staving off orgasm, he is.

When I'm not sucking on his dick, he's making me cry out. Want and lust mixed with love keep me from letting go and falling over the edge.

Because I want this feeling to last.

I want this all-consuming passion to be my past, my present, and my future.

"Oh God," I moan as he turns on the toy for what seems like the billionth time.

I'm reaching the point of no return.

Only when my balls draw up tight, my muscles ache, and my forehead sweats do I finally give in and put us both out of our misery.

When he lets me have my next break from the vibrating in my ass, I don't go back to sucking him off. Instead of putting my mouth on him, I reach for the condom.

He widens his thighs and leans back as I roll it down his hard cock. "You sure you're ready for me?"

"So ready. I've been ready since we were eighteen."

Back then, I regretted not taking this step with him sooner. We had one night where I was inside him, and I've been thinking about the alternative for years.

"Then climb up here and ride me."

He doesn't have to ask me twice.

I squirt some lube onto his cock and pull the toy out of my ass.

Then I'm on his lap. His hands roam down my back and bite into my flesh, while he leans forward and moves his mouth over my unshaven jaw and neck.

Leaning back, I reach behind me and position his cock against my hole.

We lock eyes as I sink down on him.

He fills me until I'm fully seated in his lap.

His hands sit just above my ass, moving in slow circles while I adjust to his size. The toy helped open me up, but he's a lot bigger.

We keep staring at each other, our breaths coming out in soft wisps.

A strand of loose hair falls over his face, and I tuck it behind his ears.

All the soul-searching I've done over the last few years, the traveling, the career flip-flopping, the running away from the very future I left Cash to pursue, I realize all of that happened because I've never felt more at peace than when I'm with Cash.

I don't think I'll ever feel passionate about a career. Any career. Traveling and Cash are the only things that have centered me, and choosing to go with him on tour means I can have both of them.

I don't know what I'll do for money, and I'd feel weird having Cash pay my way, but if it means becoming a luggage bitch boy for him, then at least I'll be pulling my weight.

The job doesn't matter.

Cash does.

I will never, ever make the same mistake I did when I forced us to part for the greater good.

It wasn't the greater good at all. It unnecessarily hurt us both, but try telling teenagers that they met their soul mate at seventeen years old. Neither of us would've believed it.

"I love you," I whisper softly.

Cash cracks a smile. "You're just saying that because of this." He thrusts upward, and I throw my head back in pleasure.

"Do it again," I order.

He does, and I have to grip the back of the couch behind him.

Pleasure ripples through me as his cock hits my prostate.

I lean up on my knees slightly so he can move beneath me and take what he needs.

His hips buck as he moves in and out of my hole, but he goes slow. "I can't believe we never did this back then." He sounds pained, like he's trying to hold back.

My mouth moves next to his ear. "From memory, I offered. Also, you don't need to be gentle with me. I can take it."

"I'm trying to make this last. You feel amazing."

"After all that edging, I don't need it to last. You've barely moved inside me and I'm on the edge." I kiss his cheek. "Let go, Cashton."

He lets out a groan. "Oh, God."

"Again, my name is Locke, but I guess God is okay too."

"You're *so* funny. Just for that ..." With strength neither of us had ten years ago, Cash pushes me off him and onto my back on the couch. His callused, guitar-playing hands grip my knees and push them back while his cock finds my hole again.

He does what I wanted, and he lets go. He fucks me with no hesitation.

I don't remember sex ever feeling this way.

I've had one-night stands that were great sex and no feelings. I've made love with all the feels of romance.

I've never experienced the mind-blowing sex filled with love and passion at the same time.

My head swims, my skin flushes. I break into a sweat and try to reach for my cock, but Cash swats my hand away.

"My job," he grits out.

Then his hand is there, working me over while he continues to push past my prostate time and time again.

Even though I'd love for this to go on forever, I know I'm not going to make it much longer.

The dual sensation of his hand on my dick and his cock in my ass pushes me toward the finish line like a train with no brakes.

My mouth dries, my chest heaves, and as my whole body tenses, Cash lets out a strained grunt and slows.

His hand tightens on my cock. My ass contracts around his pulsing dick.

And in one quick breath, I come apart.

Ropes of cum hit my stomach.

Cash thrusts inside me one last time, and my dick twitches. He collapses on top of me, our sweaty bodies colliding, our breathing erratic.

"Feel that?" Cash rocks his hips as he pulls out of me. He might not be inside me anymore, but he doesn't leave me. He buries his head in my neck, and I lower my legs to go around the backs of his thighs.

We stay on the small couch, wrapped in each other.

"What?" I breathe.

"The gigantic shift in the universe."

"Is that what we're calling your dick now? The universe?"

Cash laughs against my skin. "No. Ten years ago, my whole world was thrown off its axis when you left me. It's been skewed ever since." He lifts his head, and those warm brown eyes I fell in love with a long time ago stare down at me. "It's finally fixed."

I lean up and capture his mouth with mine, capturing the sweat off his top lip. It's soft and sweet.

When he pulls away and his body leaves me, I furrow my brow.

He sits up, resting on his knees between my legs.

I'm covered in cum, he's still wearing the condom, and his hair is a tangled mess.

"What's wrong?" I ask.

"Did you mean it?"

"Mean what?"

"That you'll come with me wherever I go? That we'll make this work? Or now that the need for an orgasm has subsided, are you realizing how unrealistic that is?"

My heart sinks. "Is that what's happening with you? I meant every word, but I don't know how it will work. All I know is I want to try. I can't live without you again. I just can't. I'm lost without you. I don't know who I am, nothing makes sense, and I do stupid impulsive things to try to forget you, but I can't. I won't." I sit up, almost bringing us face-to-face. I glance up at him through my lashes. "I promise I won't turn your world upside down ever again."

A tear slips down Cash's face. "No matter what?"

"No matter what."

Cash grins. "Good. Because I have a plan."

"Already?"

"You complaining?"

"Never."

He kisses me again, and I don't even need to hear his plan to be on board.

We're a team now.

Nothing will ever break us apart again.

"CASH?" Locke's sweet voice echoes around the tiles of the hotel bathroom.

I duck my head out from behind the shower curtain while the hot water beats down on my tired muscles.

My boyfriend dicked me out so hard I can barely stand, but he doesn't appear to be as happy about it as I do. He stands at the door with his hands on his hips, a hotel robe wrapped around him, and a scowl on his face.

The sweet voice was a trap. Clearly.

After convincing the band to write our next album in Vegas so Locke and I could spend more time together and Locke could work out what he wants to do with his career, I ended up asking him to be the band's financial advisor.

It made sense at the time, but I didn't think of what it would be like having a partner see every cent I spend.

"Can't hear you. Showering." I put my head back under the water, but I can still hear him.

"Cashton Evelyn Kingsley."

"That's not my name," I sing.

The shower curtain is ripped away.

"What am I in trouble for?" I ask as innocently as I can.

"Want to tell me why you dropped fifteen thousand during your shopping trip with Seb this morning?"

"You said the limit of spending without you being alerted was twenty?"

He folds his arms. "Not the point."

"I'm really beginning to regret hiring you as the band's financial manager."

"No, you're not."

I swallow hard. "I am with this."

I turn off the shower and reach for my towel, but Locke steals it away from me.

"Babe," I complain, "I love you, but now is not the time to have this conversation."

I thought I was safe spending that much. I don't even know how he found out.

"What conversation?"

I huff and grab my towel off him. "You'll find out soon."

"You didn't go and buy me a whole new wardrobe again, did you? I still have clothes with tags on them. You need to stop spending frivolously, especially on stuff for me."

"No, I don't. And it wasn't clothes. And it wasn't frivolous."

"But it was for me?"

"No." I hate my voice goes up at the end, so I make my escape into the hotel suite.

"Cashton Muriel Kingsley." He follows me.

"Why do you always give me feminine-sounding middle names?"

"Because I can." Now Locke's hands are on his hips.

He's not going to let this go.

I turn to him. "Think really hard about what you're doing, Sherlock Emerson. If you push this, it will be your fault."

"What will be my fault? Why can't you just tell me what ridiculous thing you bought me this time?"

I point at him. "Your fault."

I go to where I stashed the tiny box as soon as I got back to the hotel so Locke couldn't find it.

When I pull it out, my boyfriend's eyes widen.

"Wait ..."

"Nope." I put emphasis on the *P*. "You pushed, and now you must suffer the consequences." I step toward him. "When the tabloids ask about this moment, I will have to tell them the truth. You cornered me while I was showering and demanded I tell you my secret."

"Cashton ..." Locke covers his mouth with his hand.

I reach him and get down on one knee. "I will have to tell them I did this naked with nothing but a towel wrapped around my waist, and I will even have to mention that my cock fell out because it wanted in on the moment." I fix the towel.

"I love you so much" is all he says.

"Good. Still doesn't change this story." I hold up the box and lift the lid, revealing a platinum men's wedding band with two rows of fine diamonds around the middle.

Locke lets out a soft gasp.

"I've been planning this ever since you got the official word that your divorce was final."

I've been making *Big Plans*. Life plans. And they all involve the boy I fell in love with at seventeen years old.

I would give up my entire world for him.

He's the only thing that matters to me.

I love Seb and my other bandmates.

I love my life on the road.

But I love Locke more.

"I've been thinking about this moment since we were eighteen years old," Locke whispers.

"I have always loved you. I've never loved another. And I know I never will. Sherlock Michael Emerson, will you marry me?"

He nods, and tears fill his eyes. "Yes. Yes, I will, Cashton Olivia Kingsley."

𝄞

THE END

THORNED HEART

IT'S NEVER a good thing when I'm woken by my phone constantly going off.

What have my guys done now?

People think being a band manager is all glamor and the better parts of fame without being part of the spotlight.

They would be wrong. *So wrong*.

It's like babysitting unruly frat boys.

Not that I don't love it. I do. Especially the guys from Cash Me Outside.

They work hard and play even harder, but it's the playing part of the rock star lifestyle that makes my job an around-the-clock thing.

I reach for my phone on my bedside table and chant, "Please let Cash have run off with his fiancé to elope. Please let it be Greg or Jasper with the latest Instagram influencer. Please let this be news I don't need to get out of bed for. Anything but —" I look at my screen and deflate "—fucking Seb."

Words like "Nudes" and "Dick Pic" are splashed all over my screen.

Why does this shit always happen in the middle of the goddamn night?

I open my texts, and there are the words I really don't like seeing from anyone in the band—*I fucked up*—but with Seb, it's so much worse.

Because there's my teeny tiny issue of being totally in love with the band's lead guitarist, but that's not exactly public knowledge.

No one knows.

The nightly jerk-off sessions while thinking of Sebastian Rose will always be my dirty little secret.

I've been a pillar of professionalism with each and every member of the band and don't mention my love life to them at all. Hell, I don't think they even know I'm bi. They've only seen me with women because I refuse to be a headline in entertainment news by taking a guy to any official events. I'm not going to come out and overshadow the band like that.

Also, I would never go there with a client. Not unless I knew it was going to be for real, and Seb doesn't do real. Or serious. Or, hell, even temporary. He gives a new meaning to the phrase one-and-done. With him, it's one-and-don't-let-the-door-hit-your-ass-on-the-way-out. And that's exactly how he gets himself in situations like this.

I stumble out of bed and put on sweats and a T-shirt, and then look at the calendar in my phone to work out what city we're in and open the notes section to where I put the guys' room numbers.

Okay, room 1406.

I'm out the door and in the elevator as fast as humanly possible. Only then do I let myself look at the leaked pictures so I know what I'm working with.

I've seen Seb in many states of undress. I've seen him

getting a blowjob for fuck's sake. For a while, he'd used me to get rid of his hookups after he was done, and I was more than happy to kick out the men he was sharing his bed with. Until I wasn't anymore.

The more it happened, the angrier I got about not being the one on my knees for him.

I'd started interrupting earlier and earlier until it got to the point neither of them had gotten off yet. That only happened a couple of times before Seb stopped messaging me that he was going home with someone.

Maybe I shouldn't have let my jealous side come out to play because if I hadn't, maybe we wouldn't be in this predicament. He would've texted me that he was with someone, and I could've interrupted and sent the jerk packing.

I wouldn't be looking at very hot photos of a naked, *sleeping* Seb. They simultaneously turn me on while making me ragey. I turn my phone to the side. *Dayyymn*, his body is perfection.

Whoever sold these photos to TMZ deserves to have their nuts chopped off. I'd put them in a blender and make him a testicle smoothie with his own balls. Motherfucker, whoever it is.

There are two things working in Seb's favor though. From a management perspective anyway. One, he has nothing to be ashamed about in the cock department. Even soft, it's long and *mouthwatering*. Two, he's a guy. A rock star no less. He's openly gay, he doesn't have a partner or husband, so the tabloids can't claim he's cheating, and the only scandal here is the photos themselves. This won't do anything but boost his popularity.

Don't get me started on the double standards between men and women in this industry. If Seb was a female, there'd be slut-shaming everywhere.

The only thing I'm worried about with this is Seb's mental state. Seb's tough on the outside. A snarky pain in my ass. He only shows his true side to the band, and even then, I don't think Jasper and Greg get to see *everything*. He reserves that for his best friend Cash, the lead singer of the band, and occasionally me, but I have to catch him in a vulnerable moment for it to happen.

The only time I see the real him is when he's too drained and exhausted to hide it. I've seen him in some emotional states over the last few years that have made my heart hurt for him.

He's an artist.

He's a songwriter.

He creates emotional music.

But all of that is wrapped up in a fuckboy rock star who doesn't give a shit about anything but performing and getting laid.

I knock on his door, and a small voice answers.

"No."

I huff a laugh. "No?"

"I don't want to let you in." He knew it was me.

That makes me happy even though it shouldn't.

This is vulnerable Seb, not rock star Seb, and I just want to get in there so I can hold him and assure him everything's okay.

I place my hand on his suite's door. "You're not in trouble."

"I don't believe you."

The door cracks open and Seb's dark eyes meet mine. His long brown frizzy hair is messy, his beard untamed.

"Can I come in?" I don't give him a chance to respond. I push my way inside the hotel room.

Seb's shirtless, the bedsheets are crumpled, and the lighting in the room is dim. I can picture Seb's big body in that bed, naked and writhing. The leaked image pops into my head, and I wince. I shouldn't be thinking about Seb that way, but the photo doesn't help me remember that.

Okay, time to get to business. "So, that text you sent."

"I had no idea he took photos." He has this panic to his voice I hate hearing from him. "If I did—"

"Hey, shh." I step forward and rub his arms, but he refuses to lift his head to look at me. "I meant why do you think you fucked up when this is not your fault? Wait, how did you even find out about it? I'm usually the bearer of bad news when it comes to everything tabloid related."

"I couldn't sleep, so I was on my socials, and my phone started lighting up with tags."

"I told you to delete those."

"I get bored when insomnia hits."

"There are healthier apps to go on than social media. You *know* that."

Seb sighs. "I do. But it's addictive."

I can't even fault him. When you're a public figure, all those likes, shares, and comments are like crack, but there's the ugly side to fame too, and Seb faces more than his fair share of bigots expressing their toxic opinions.

That might be another downfall to this—the comments about him being a gross *gay* guy who clearly has just finished having big bad *gay sex* with a *man* in the pictures—but it won't be much different to the comments he usually gets on that front.

He hasn't looked at me yet, so I lift his chin.

"Seb?"

Those almost black eyes pierce through me.

"It's not your fault. What this guy did—whoever he is—he is responsible. Who is he?"

He steps out of my hold. "That's where I fucked up."

"You didn't get a name." There's an edge to my voice, but shit, Seb's not a regular person. He can't do regular people hookups, and this is exactly why.

I don't ask him much. If he'd caught the guy's name, I could track down the source of the original photo and sue the fuck out of him.

"I got it," Seb says sheepishly. "I just … forgot what it was."

I pull up the photo again. "When was this?"

"A few weeks ago."

"Can you remember the exact date or venue?" I try to match the photo of the hotel room to my memory of what damn city that was, but we're on the tail end of the US tour and have seen the inside of sixty venues in the past few months. They all blur together after a while. "San Antonio maybe?" I think I remember that particular headboard in Texas.

"I'm sorry, Thorne."

I plaster on my smile that I give the guys when I don't have great news. "Hey, this is not going to affect you or the band. I'm more worried how you're taking it."

Seb shrugs with a trademark smirk. "I have nothing to be embarrassed about. I have an *amazing* cock." And there's the fuckboy everyone thinks he is.

"You don't have to do that with me, you know."

"Do what?"

"Deflect your feelings with that armor of yours."

Seb holds strong, but it doesn't last. When he sees how serious I am, he deflates faster than a balloon. "You really want to know how I feel? Fuck that guy. Fuck everyone who has already shared that pic. Fuck all of them."

I want to make this better for him, but I can't. "Maybe look at it like that photo shoot you did for Out Artist magazine before the tour. You were naked for that."

"That was tasteful, and my junk was mostly covered. I also *consented* to that. I don't care about the image. It's how it got out there that I'm pissed about."

"I know. I'm sorry."

"It was an intimate moment, and yeah, a lot of my hookups have been cheap and probably nasty, but this … this makes me feel so small and insignificant. It makes me feel *dirty*, and I usually like that."

I try not to think about what kind of dirty things Seb likes.

He goes to the edge of his bed and sits, running his hands through his long locks. "I've messed up a lot over the years, but not like this. This is next level."

"I don't want to say I told you so, but I do recall telling you to stop with the groupies." Okay, so I might have had ulterior motives for telling him that, but this proves I had a point anyway.

"Maybe I should."

I throw my hands up in victory. "He finally gets it. Only took leaked nudes."

He scowls at me, and fuck, it's cute.

"Sorry. Too soon?" I ask.

"Way too soon."

"I'll handle this, okay? I might not be able to get the source of the photo, but we can bury it and try to get people to stop sharing it." I turn to leave.

"Wait, now?" He stands.

"The sooner I get onto it, the more chance we have of killing it."

"What if … what if we just ignore it?"

I frown. "You want me to let it go?"

"I … I don't want to be alone right now."

I'm surprised by Seb's admission, and I think I'm not the only one.

His eyes widen, and he scrambles for an explanation. "I mean, I'm scared I'll tweet something or say something and make it worse. I need supervision."

I'm torn. I should go and deal with this, but when Seb asks me for something, it's next to impossible for me to say no.

"I can get one of the other guys to come down. Maybe Cash and Locke can babysit you while I get to work."

"No, don't bother them when they're in their love bubble."

"Jasper? Greg?"

Seb shakes his head. "I want you."

Holy shit.

Holy. Fucking. Shit.

He should not say things like that to me.

I move closer to him. "Are you sure?"

"You know how to deal with my shit better than anyone I know."

Which is exactly why I should not get in his bed. The way he's looking at me right now—he's looking for someone to comfort him. I don't know if I can handle being the guy he needs right now. Not when I'm that close to him.

"I can't deal with your problem if I'm in here with you though."

Seb closes his eyes and lets out a loud breath. "I want to hit pause on the world for a bit."

As easy as that, I know I'll give him what he wants. There's no way I can say no. I tentatively climb into bed next to him and lie on the edge as far away from his side as I can get. "Let's try to get some sleep, and I'll deal with this in the morning, okay? If the label asks, I slept through the ten billion notifications I have on my phone."

"Thank you," he whispers.

I turn my head toward him. "No problem. Anything for my client. You know that."

Yes, Thorne. Your *client*.

Remember that.

CLIENT. I hate when Thorne calls me that.

His blue eyes don't look at me like I'm only a client. They're soft and kind. His other features—his hard square jaw and his always meticulously neat blond hair—aren't as welcoming, but his eyes … they give away the kindness under his stoic façade.

Most days it feels like Thorne is one of us, like maybe we're friends—*close* friends—but every now and then he throws the client label at me, and I'm reminded he's only here because we pay him.

I should let him go do his thing, but … I can't be alone. I just … can't.

Normally, I'd turn to Cash with this shit. He understands it because he's been there. Okay, he hasn't had dick pics leaked, but he's had personal moments splashed all over the media.

Like the time he wanted to win over Locke and declared his love in public. Viral videos and photos of that moment were everywhere. And yes, Cash voluntarily did it in front of all those people, which is a lot different than a post-sex photo taken without my permission, but Cash would still understand better than anyone. I don't want to put this on him though. Ever since he reunited with his high school sweetheart, I haven't wanted to take away from Cash's happiness with industry bullshit.

And this is complete bullshit.

I remember the guy who did this. I might be blanking on his name, but I remember his face and the cute little smile he had that now looks more sinister than playful in my mind. The memory of him leaving is vague. I swear I told him to let himself out, and then ... shit, I guess I let my guard down and fell asleep before he actually left?

That part is fuzzy.

I learned early on in this industry not to trust anyone, so I never let them stay the night, but I do kind of suck at kicking them out. I've been getting better but obviously I fucked up with this guy.

Who the fuck takes a photo of someone while they're sleeping and sells it for the world to see?

This isn't like paparazzi photos or fans taking photos when they see us on the street.

I've never felt as used as I do right now, like I've sold my body without permission.

Do I really care my cock is out there for everyone's viewing pleasure? Not really. My dick isn't the point. It's *amazing* but not the point.

It's the consent.

The *violation*.

The idea that my body belongs to everyone simply because I'm famous.

"I wonder how much your cock is worth," Thorne says out of nowhere.

It's weird being next to him even though it's not the first time we've shared a bed. This is different than the tour bus bed where we'd take it in shifts to get sleep and had no other choice but to share with someone.

This is ... more intimate.

I shake that thought free because I can't afford to think like that.

"Wow, if you didn't have a comeback for that, you must really be frazzled."

I turn my head. "What?"

"I asked how much you think your cock is worth. *Priceless, a billion dollars*, or *more than you can afford* didn't come out of your mouth immediately." Thorne is stoic and serious most of the time, but every now and then he'll let his guard down and make a joke.

I laugh. "I didn't need to say it because you already knew what I was thinking."

Under the covers, a hand brushes over mine. "Try not to think about it and get some sleep, okay?"

"Okay."

Thorne tries to pull his hand away, but I hold tight. It's warm in my palm and gives me a sense that everything will be all right.

Like Thorne says, this is nothing. Tomorrow, they'll bury it, and everything will be fixed.

I begin to drift off with images of that nameless guy taking photos of me. A few times, I startle awake, thinking he's standing at the end of my bed, but Thorne's right there, still holding my hand, and I fall asleep again.

I don't know how long for though. Harsh whispers filter into my subconscious at one point, and I partially open one eye and see a blue light from a screen. I squeeze the hand that ... oh. Thorne's gone.

At least, I think he is. I open my eyes fully and find him sitting next to me. His laptop has appeared from nowhere which means he left me at one point, but now he's back, talking on the phone and tapping away on his computer.

"Thorne?" I croak.

He flinches and almost knocks his laptop off his lap. Then it's a scramble to end his phone call as fast as possible. "Sorry. I didn't mean to wake you."

"What are you doing?"

Thorne reaches over and runs a hand through my hair.

I tell myself not to read into it. It's his job to coddle us in these types of situations.

"I'm fixing this," he whispers. "I promise you."

I don't have the energy to fight it. "Okay."

Sleep pulls me under once more.

$\oint$

When actual morning arrives and I wake properly, I think I have to be dreaming.

Thorne is pressed against me. Well, technically, I'm pressed against him. He's on his back, and I'm curled into his side with my head in the nook of his shoulder. My leg is over his waist, and his morning wood presses against my thigh. Mine digs into his hip.

I have the urge to rut against him and keep going until I come, but I won't.

Because one, this is *Thorne*. And two, falling asleep and accidentally cuddling means nothing.

Clearly, I tried to cling to him in my incapacitated state,

and he was either out of it after being up half the night trying to fix my mess or he was feeling sorry for me and let it happen.

For a moment, I sink into his warmth and pretend like this could be my life. Waking up cuddled with a man who I actually like, who isn't using me because of who I am, and who's someone I genuinely admire. Thorne would make the perfect partner—you know, if he wasn't straight. I don't have a thing for Thorne but the idea of him. He's hot, he doesn't take my shit, and I can trust him. *And* he's nice when it matters.

He's always so good to me even though I make his job more complicated. Since Cash got engaged, the tabloids have followed me around hoping for a fuck up.

Well, I certainly gave them what they wanted.

Cash is boring to them now he's in a committed relationship. He's still in the media plenty, but it's not because of a scandal. And scandals sell.

Evidently, my cock is scandalous.

I don't want to wake up properly and face the day. I want to stay here in Thorne's warmth and live the fantasy of a normal life for a little longer.

Bang, bang, bang, bang, bang.

Knew it was too good to last.

"Open up." It's Cash.

Thorne doesn't stir in my arms. He's too out of it.

I roll out of bed, and Thorne moans but still doesn't wake. Stumbling toward the hotel room door, I pull it open and stare at my best friend through squinted eyes.

Fuck, the hallway's bright.

I rub the back of my neck, but the mess that is my hair falls over my face. I try to tame the mane, but it's too fucked up. Unlike Cash, who has long straight hair, mine is a nest of curls and frizz.

"Dude, have you seen—" Cash lets himself in and pauses. "Holy shit, did you fuck our manager?"

Locke, Cash's fiancé, steps through after him. He's a tall, kind of lanky redhead with freckles. Definitely not the image of someone who a rock star would be marrying, but he makes Cash happy, and that's all that matters.

"Good morning, Cash," Thorne rumbles and sits up.

His gray T-shirt sits tight across his impressive chest, and since when do I notice Thorne's chest?

I shake my head.

Get a grip, Seb.

"Awkward," Locke says.

"How long has this been going on?" Cash asks.

I roll my eyes. "He crashed in here last night after the awesomeness that is my dick has been released into the world. Did you know that it's so impressive it can be seen from space? Cockgate is a *huge* scandal. What can I say? I love making Thorne's job hard."

"That makes more sense." Cash glances between Thorne and me. "And, uh, that's why I'm down here. I was wondering if you'd seen the news."

"The news being my dick? Yes, I see it every day. And it's *big* news."

Cash holds up his hand. "Okay, we get it. You're delusional about the size of your dick."

I force a grin. Playing it off, I can do this.

Thorne stands and stretches. "We have one more show before we have a break for Christmas. How about we try not to make the news today?"

"We promise," Cash and I say at the same time in a monotone voice.

Thorne waves a finger between us. "I don't like it when you two do that. It usually means you're faking it."

Cash throws up his hands. "Hey, I'm not the troublemaker anymore thanks to this guy." He pulls Locke close.

I want someone to pull close to me.

I've never had that before, and I don't know why I suddenly need it. Could it be that I've reached that age where people want to settle down? Or is it I see how happy Locke makes Cash, and I realize how empty my life is?

It's rock star tours and partying and sex. So. Much. Sex. But I don't have that emotional connection to anyone. Or *anything*.

I don't know how I'm supposed to find that while doing what we do. I don't have a high school sweetheart out there somewhere hoping I come find them.

Thorne grips my shoulder. "Seb?"

I blink out of my daze and am met with three concerned stares. "What?"

"We asked if you were ready for breakfast." Cash cocks his head.

"Oh. Right. Breakfast. Yup. Let me just ..." I pick up the nearest clothes lying on the floor and throw them on.

The hotel we're staying at is super nice. Way too nice for a rock tour who are more likely to trash their five-star furnishings. That's probably why they gave us one of their small conference rooms to use as the band and crew's breakfast buffet.

We go down there as a group, and while I'm used to people staring at me—well, I'm used to people staring at Cash who's always beside me—this is different. As soon as we enter the room, every set of eyes are on me, and I have to play the part.

The voice inside my head screams *run*, but I can't do that.

I wave everyone off, though it looks more like a flail.

"Please, like half of you hadn't already seen my cock."
Everyone in the room bursts into laughter. "Didn't realize it
was that funny," I mumble.

Cash nudges me. "Water off a duck's back, am I right?"

"Sure."

We load up our plates from the portable chafing dishes, but
when we go to find seats, there are none. I want to make it an
excuse so I can take my plate back to the room, but as usual,
our crew moves for us to take seats at the table. The one time I
don't want to be treated like a celebrity, they move.

Right.

Of course.

This is fine.

We'll do the concert tonight, fly to bumfuck Montana
tomorrow to spend Christmas together in a secluded cabin
owned by some dude Cash knows, and by the time we go back
on tour in the new year, this whole thing will be forgotten.

It's fine.

Everything is ... fine.

EVERYTHING IS NOT FINE.

I can tell.

It's our last show for the US tour, finishing where we started in LA, but something's wrong. The spark Seb usually brings to the stage is missing.

Seb's fingers move expertly while he plays his guitar, he sings the right notes, but he's not himself. To the unknowing eye, he's doing his thing, and he's killing it. But it's as if he's dying on the inside while he does it.

That's not Seb.

I'm watching from my usual spot—in the wings, always on Seb's side.

The band finishes a song, and I lift my fingers to my mouth to let out a loud whistle. He hears me, and his dark eyes meet mine. There's always arrogance shining in them, but tonight, it's missing. All I see is a cautious and timid person.

I don't want to be insensitive to whatever he's going through, but I have to wonder if there's something more than the photo. The fallout today hasn't been *that* bad. Tonight's concert started with wolf-whistles and mockery, which wasn't great. Some of the crew have made snarky comments, and there's been some online chatter and sharing. But a lot of the fanbase and industry people have come to Seb's defense, blasting those on social media who have shared the image.

The thing I've noticed with working in this industry for fifteen years is fans don't understand that famous people are human too. They're not hard shells who can drown all the negativity out, and when their privacy is violated—which it is a lot—they're told to suck it up and stop being so sensitive.

Thick skin is a requirement, definitely, but everyone has weak moments. *Everyone.* And in the four years I've been working for this band, Seb hasn't broken once.

I want to be his rock.

Spending the night with him, just holding his hand and falling asleep next to him has blurred that professional line more than ever before.

I've been so good for so long, but watching Seb struggle, it's taking every ounce of strength I have to hold myself back. I don't know how I'm going to be able to keep this wall between us these next two weeks while we're holed up in the snow.

Last I heard, Jasper and Greg are planning to bring groupies with them to fill the time. Cash will have Locke.

Seb and I ...

Shit, I can't break my rules no matter how much I want to.

Last night when he inched his way over to my side of the bed and cuddled into me, I let it happen even though I shouldn't have. He was asleep and not aware of what he was doing. Nothing about it was sexual, but it was more intimate than any sex act I've ever experienced, and now my ridiculous obsession with him is moving into dangerous territory.

I know how easy it would've been to turn it into sex. I've

thought about how many different ways I could break my rules. I'd know exactly what to say and how to say it. I'd know what to do to get him into bed because, let's be honest, it wouldn't be that hard.

Hell, I've seen him exchange a single look with a fan and then got the text later to kick the guy out of his room for him. He's easy, to put it mildly, but I don't want to be just some fuck to him.

If I was to ever put my job on the line, it would have to be for more than one night of sex. I'd want him to become mine.

The set is almost finished, and in between songs, some jackass down the front yells at Seb to take off his pants. He ignores them and plays like the professional he is, but my heart hurts for him.

The guys finish their setlist with the usual pyrotechnics that go off at their finales. They love ending a show with a bang, and this tour is no exception. In fact, I'm pretty sure this is the most expensive fireworks display any band has ever done in the history of rock, and that's saying something. There are fire balls, and all sorts of shit flying around the stage. I'm honestly surprised no one's been hurt yet.

But whenever I've tried to tell Cash that maybe it's a wee bit too much, he puts on his dramatic voice and says, "It's theater, darling." Then laughs because he thinks he's so damn hilarious.

After the over the top display, Seb pushes past me like a man on a mission, taking his guitar with him even though the case for it is right by my side.

"Seb?"

He waves me off.

"What about the encore?" I call after him.

He doesn't stop.

Cash steps in front of me. "Is he okay? He was out of it for half the show."

So Cash noticed too. I was hoping I was reading into everything because I'm worried about him.

I glance in the direction Seb disappeared to. "I honestly don't know."

"I guess I'm playing for this encore then." Cash goes to one of Seb's backup guitars.

"You got this?" I ask him.

"You know it. Can you go make sure he's okay?"

"Already ahead of you." I push my way through the crowd of backstage crew and roadies, hoping like hell Seb's gone to the dressing room.

I walk in to find him changing out of his pants.

His bare ass and exposed muscles in his wide back and shoulders are right there, and I should not be imagining pushing him against the nearest wall and fucking him until he forgets all his problems. But now my brain's already on that track, and my cock gets on board too.

I only manage to shake out of my daze when he pulls on some jeans and throws a clean T-shirt over his head.

"What time's the flight to Montana?" he asks.

I meet his eyes, and if he caught me staring, he doesn't acknowledge it. His dark eyes are colder than usual, and that same vibe of him not really being himself is still there.

"Are you okay?" I ask.

"Peachy. I just … I need to be on my own for a bit. So, what time's the flight?"

"Need to be in the charter terminal in two hours."

"I'll be there." Seb goes to walk past me when I grab his arm.

"Will you, though?"

"I promise."

I don't want to let him go because I get the feeling he's lying, but there's absolutely no reason for me, professionally, to hold him back.

This vacation was a choice. With Cash's mom retired and traveling overseas, Locke's parents not speaking to him, and my family scattered across the country, we decided to spend Christmas together. Seb has parents he could go home to. So do Jasper and Greg, but they figured two weeks of secluded living would give us all a break from the full-speed lives we lead.

I don't know how I'm supposed to let him go and just hope that he turns up later. I'm worried he's going to go out and do something stupid and that will only make this situation worse.

We have the PR team at Joystar Records doing damage control and getting the photo buried on all social media sites. Another scandal so close could bring them back up to the surface. Next thing we know, Seb will be having a diva-inspired meltdown and attacking paparazzi. The last thing he needs to do is add fuel to this fire.

But I can't keep him with me like some hostage, and I can't follow where he goes because arguably, that's not my job. I reluctantly release his arm, but I stop him right before he walks out that door.

"Seb?"

He pauses.

"Please don't do anything stupid."

"I wouldn't be me if I promised that." The forced smile on his face says more than his words do.

I fear what's coming next. If he even shows up at the airport at all.

𝄞

It's worse than I'm expecting. Worse than worse.

I thought at most Seb would blow off the band vacation and disappear on some bender and meet us in LA before we fly out for the Australasian leg of the tour.

This? Yeah, this is definitely worse than that. Because he walks through the doors of the private charter terminal with a half-naked twink on his arm.

This *boy* is wearing silver boots, silver boy shorts, and a giant gray fur coat. Nothing else. He has a pretty face, blond hair ... and his tiny hands all over my ... Seb.

"Hey, everyone. This is ... Andrew."

Could be worse. Could've been something like Butterfly or Sugarbits.

"But my stage name is Lemon, and everyone calls me that."
There it is.

I'm not bitter. Not bitter at all.

"He's decided to come with us," Seb says.

I grunt. "Packing light, are we?" Yes, that's a dig at Lemon's size and pointing out the fact he doesn't have a bag and I'm pretty sure in the middle of Montana in December, he's going to die of hypothermia. Or lose his dick to frostbite.

Is it bad karma to wish that on someone?

"He can wear my clothes," Seb says.

"Or none at all," Lemon supplies unhelpfully.

He's definitely going to die of hypothermia.

I can see the headlines now. Naked, Malnourished Twink Dies in Snow Because Cash Me Outside's Lead Guitarist is a Slut.

That's probably too long for a headline but whatever.

This Christmas is going to be the best. I'm alone, and the guy I'm in love with is with someone else. No matter how temporary they are together, it still fucking hurts.

"Lemon." I try to smile though I'm gritting my teeth. "See the desk over there? Can you please go let them know your name and show your ID so they can put you on the flight manifesto? Thank you so much."

Seb's eyes narrow at me. "Isn't that your job?"

"I would do it, but I need a word with you." I cock my brow at him.

"Fine." He turns to Lemon. "You good?"

"I can manage my name. Go talk to your ... Dad?"

The entire band bursts out laughing. That's going to be a fun ongoing joke that will die, oh probably never.

Seb walks over to me, but I drag him into the corner of the small waiting lounge so no one can hear us.

"This is your definition of not doing something stupid?" I hiss. "I guarantee sleeping with that ... boy would be the literal meaning of *doing something stupid*."

"That's not nice. You don't even know Andrew."

"*Lemon*."

"Yeah, I'm not calling him that."

"Where did you even meet him?"

"Uh ..." Seb rubs the back of his neck. "Strip club? Maybe?"

I pinch the bridge of my nose. "Please don't tell me you're bringing a hooker to our vacation in Montana."

"He's not a hooker. He's a stripper, and I'm not *paying* him to be here. He recognized me and fanboyed all over me."

"Mm, fanboyed all over your lap, maybe."

"Why is this a problem? Jasper and Greg are bringing randos."

"Normally, I wouldn't give a fuck who's in your bed." *Lies.* "But isn't this the entire reason you're in the tabloids right now with your dick out?"

"Oh yeah. That reminds me. Can we get him to sign, like, an NDA or something?"

Jesus H Christ.

"What are you doing, Seb? Really?"

"I'm spending my Christmas vacation with a guy who has the potential to be more than a hookup."

I almost fall over. "Come again?"

Seb waggles his eyebrows. "That's what he'll be saying later."

I wince. "What the fuck?"

"What?"

He really has no idea.

"You want more … than a hookup? Are you okay and should I be taking you to the hospital instead of on vacation?"

"Ha, ha."

"No, seriously."

Seb sighs, and I feel a pull of sympathy for him. "I don't know, okay? I'm happy for Cash, but him getting together with Locke, and the photo thing … I'm sick of being used, you know? And, okay, yes, I'm sick of using people too. It goes both ways. I want something …" He glances over at Cash who's sitting on his fiancé's lap. "I want what they have."

If I'd known a leaked dick pic would make him get to this point, I might have done it myself two years ago when my feelings for him started to change.

It had been weeks of him texting me to come help get rid of his one-night stands from his hotel room. Every time I'd do it, I'd feel … ick. There was something stirring in my gut. I told myself for months that it was because he was degrading my job, but deep down I knew it wasn't. It was because I hated the thought of him with someone else.

"Do you really think *Lemon* is your future?" I ask.

"No, but *Andrew* could be. I've never actually *tried* before."

Try with me, I want to scream.

I want to yell at him for being blind because the only reason Lemon is here is for a free vacation with a rock star.

He probably doesn't even care to get to know Seb. He won't be stage side, watching him play, watching his moods, and wanting to make him feel better when he's going through shit.

But it's better for Seb to learn that shit on his own.

"Okay, he can stay. But you have to give it a real shot. I will not bail you out the minute you realize you have nothing in common and he's only here for one thing. You have to make him leave on your own."

"I promise. I'm getting better at kicking them out."

I cock my head. "Do I need to pull up the photo again of you sleeping because you forgot to kick someone out of your bed?"

"Fine. Touché. Whatever. It's going to be different with Andrew."

"Lemon," I mutter as he walks off.

He definitely hears me though because he shakes his head.

Seb wants a relationship? I never thought I'd see the day. I didn't even know *relationship* was in his vocabulary.

And now it's here, I get to watch it all unfold because I'm too chickenshit to tell him how I feel. There's too much at stake to offer myself as his relationship guinea pig. Which means, I have to continue to keep my mouth shut.

If seeing him hook up with someone was hard enough, I really don't want to think about what watching him fall in love will do to me.

WE BOARD THE PRIVATE PLANE, and Andrew immediately tries to climb into my lap. I wrap my long, guitar-playing fingers around his narrow hips and push him onto the seat next to me.

He pouts. "What, no mile-high club stuff?"

My dick gives a little twitch, but that's about it. "It's the law we all have to be in our seats for takeoff and landing." I'm relieved when Andrew stops touching me to fasten his seatbelt.

Relief isn't what I should be feeling, so that's not a good sign.

I went out tonight trying to find someone to fuck. To try to get out of my head. But then it somehow turned into projections of finding my own Locke.

Cash found his soul mate when he was seventeen years old. They were apart for a long time, but they made their way back. I've never felt anything like that.

The chance of going out and finding it in a stripper is slim to none, but when that photo was leaked, my sense of control slipped. I had no control over that situation. This one I do.

My gaze finds Thorne's who's sitting opposite us, and he's using that judging stare I'm used to seeing from him, and it's as if I can read his thoughts.

Ready to back out yet? We haven't left the tarmac.

He thinks I can't do this. I can't try to have a proper relationship. And now he's all but said he won't get rid of Andrew for me, I'm doubly stubborn about making this a great vacation. One where I can fall in love.

Real love.

I want to be able to go to sleep next to someone and not worry about them posting a photo of me naked. I want to be able to not worry about them going to the tabloids to tell them about "My one night with Sebastian Rose" where they claim I serenaded them with a Cash Me Outside song while I was balls deep inside them.

Totally false.

Because that would be creepy as fuck.

Maybe they imagined it because they *wanted* me to sing to them.

Thorne gives us an assessing gaze and then focuses on Andrew. "So, Lemon. You're a stripper? Paying your way through college?" He mutters under his breath, "Or high school?"

"Nope," Lemon ... Dammit, *Andrew*, says gleefully. "I just like doing it."

"Sex positivity," I say. "I like that. You'd know what that is if you ever got laid, Thorne."

"It must be good money." Thorne takes another jab while our flight attendant brings him his usual scotch on the rocks.

Andrew smiles like Thorne's implication isn't intrusive as

fuck. "It's not rock star money or anything, but I can earn anywhere between one to two grand on a good night."

Thorne's drink goes everywhere as he almost chokes on it. "A *night*?"

"Five nights a week. I do okay."

Thorne does the math quickly in his head. "Fifteen hundred on average times five, that's almost four hundred thousand a year."

I snort. "Isn't that more than what we pay you?"

Andrew giggles. "Don't tell the IRS. I don't think prison orange would suit me."

"Orange is the new lemon," I quip.

The flight is only a couple of hours, and it's in the wee hours of early morning, so the cabin is quiet, but I can feel Thorne's stare on me the whole time. I understand he's disappointed in my actions, but geez, he's making me all self-conscious and shit.

Which is why when Andrew pulls a blanket over us and reaches for my cock, my first instinct is to swat it away.

"Sorry," I whisper. "Just ... not here, okay?"

He looks confused but nods.

"Are you tired? You should sleep." I open my arms so he can lie across the seats and put his head in my lap instead.

"Thank you. You're sweeter than I thought you'd be," he whispers.

Yeah, I might have a reputation for being the complete opposite of how I'm acting, and not that long ago, I probably would've accepted a silent handjob in front of my bandmates, but I want this to be different. I *need* this to be different.

I mindlessly run my fingers through Andrew's bleached blond hair while he rests, and I throw my head back on the seat rest to try to get in some sleep too, but it's useless. Because that stare. I lift my head and meet Thorne's eyes.

Fuck, those blue orbs are intense.

I can feel everything he's putting out. Anger. Disappointment. I don't have the energy to fight him though.

He glances down at Andrew, and I swear his eyes turn green with jealousy, but that can't be right.

My cock responding to that thought and not the dude's head in my lap is also mystifying. When Thorne's eyes roam back up toward my face, something passes between us.

I don't know what, but it's confusing. I've never seen Thorne in this light. I don't even think I've seen him rattled. There's something definitely there, though.

Or I'm mentally exhausted from the last twenty-four hours, and I'm projecting crazy thoughts because maybe, just maybe, Thorne is the closest thing I have to a stabilizing figure in my life.

Thorne's lips part, as if he's about to say something, but then a feminine giggle from the back of the plane sounds, and our connection, or whatever it is, is gone.

I turn in my seat to find Jasper taking his groupie up on her offer to get freaky on the plane, unlike me. We ignore the shenanigans going on back there and pretend it's not happening.

Being on the road with these guys, we've all seen our fair share of sexcapades and wild shit. We learned fast to ignore what each other was doing, but hearing Jasper and his random girl for two weeks reminds me of the life I just promised Thorne I'm trying to give up.

Sleep eludes me, and I'm exhausted by the time we land in Montana. Dawn is breaking in the distance, and there's a team of people waiting for us in what has to be the smallest private airfield in the US.

They take our bags and lead us to the Escalades we've rented.

As soon as the doors open, and the icy air hits us, we all gasp.

"Oh holy mother of *my nuts are now inside my body*," Andrew hisses. "Maybe I should have gone home to pack some clothes?"

"I'll buy you some."

We rush to get into the awaiting cars.

Thorne gets in the driver's seat of ours, while Andrew and I take the very back row and Cash and Locke are in the middle.

The other four get into the second SUV.

"Where actually is this place?" I ask Cash.

"In a valley near Lone Mountain."

I frown. "We're heading to the middle of nowhere Montana. Are you sure this owner dude isn't going to kill us?"

Cash laughs. "He's an ex-boy bander from Eleven. The worst he might do is kill us with his horrible boy band dance moves."

"Ooh, I love Eleven." Andrew bounces next to me. "Which one is it?"

Cash looks at Andrew, and I know that expression. His brow is furrowed, and his lips are pursed. He's trying to decide whether to lie or tell the truth. "It doesn't matter because he told me he won't be there anyway."

I sit up straighter. "How did you get tangled up with Eleven? Where was I when that happened?"

Cash turns to me. "Remember when we met them, like, years ago through that Joystar benefit concert?"

I try to remember.

"Actually, come to think of it, I don't think you stayed long after our set. Anyway, their people gave Thorne all their contact details. It's how I got Ryder to produce the vocals on our Bleeding Heart album."

"So, it's Ryder?" Andrew asks.

"Nope. Anyway, I'm kinda friends with all of them, and I may or may not have blackmailed my way into scoring this cabin for the two weeks. He's been hiding out here for almost two years, and no one's found him yet."

"Blackmailed?" I ask.

"Yeah, you know, big boy band breakup, blah, blah, drama, blah. The others from Eleven are looking for him. I miiiight have used that to my advantage."

I smile at my best friend. "I'm getting worried. You make us play Katy Perry at concerts, you've befriended a boy band. You're not trying to turn us into a pop band, are you?"

Cash doesn't answer for way too long for my liking. "Nah, your ugly mug couldn't pull off pop."

"Fuck off, I can pull off everything." Though I'm sure they'd want me to shave my beard and cut my hair if that was the case.

"Oh, so you're open to putting some pop on the next album?" Cash asks.

"I take it back. I'm too ugly to be pop."

The plows must've been through in the middle of the night, because as the sun rises over the snowy land, a blanket of white surrounds the singular road driving through the hilly terrain.

As we drive around the winding roads, the picture outside the windows is one of beauty. A snow-capped mountain in the distance with sunlight breaking over the peak. The stillness of dawn and no one else on the road adds to the ambiance.

It's ... peaceful.

This vacation is exactly what I need.

We reach a large gate, and Thorne opens the driver's side window and punches in a code.

Andrew shivers at the frigid air filling the car. He has his fur jacket on, but his legs are completely bare.

I pull them into my lap and rub them, trying to warm them up.

"We're here," Thorne grumbles from upfront, but we're not moving. He scowls at me in the mirror. I raise my eyebrows.

Whatever stare-off we're having, he ends it first and goes back to the road.

The house is what feels like miles from the gated entry, and when I say house, I'm putting it mildly.

I let out a whistle as the wooden structure comes into view.

It's not a cabin. In no world could this monstrosity be called a cabin.

"Holy shit," I whisper as we climb out of the car.

"Holy shit is right," Andrew says. "It's freezing." He bypasses looking at the amazing view and heads straight for the front door.

"Not bad, huh?" Cash nudges me. "I'll go let your toy in before he freezes all the important parts you'll need to have fun with him."

I grin like I can't wait because that's how I *should* be feeling. Instead, I can't stop regretting disappointing Thorne. I don't know why this is different to any other time I've done it, but it is.

Maybe it's because he stayed up most of the night when my scandal hit trying to fix it, and this is how I repay him.

Is this what it's like to mature and grow a conscience? Can't say I'm a fan.

"Everyone grab your own bags," Thorne calls out. "We're all on vacation which means none of your asses are celebrities here. We all pull our own weight."

I take my bag out of the trunk and breathe in the mountain air, but Thorne is doing that disapproving stare again, so I hurry across the slick driveway and rush into the house.

Then I run into Andrew. Literally. He's, like, glued to my side.

"Where's our room?" He's way too excited.

"Master's off-limits to all of us," Cash says. "But all the others are up for grabs."

Andrew takes my hand. "Let's go."

I follow him and go up a set of stairs. He doesn't give me a chance to admire the house. It's all wooden paneling and glass windows, high ceilings with diagonal harsh angles, and it's a complete architect's dream.

He drags me down the hall to the last room on the left.

Floor to ceiling windows on two walls look out toward the mountain and into nature.

Warm colors, our own fireplace and private bathroom … it's perfect.

I double check the closet to make sure this isn't the master suite because it's the most amazing room I've ever stepped foot in, and that's saying something. We've stayed in the best hotels in the world. This shits all over that.

The room is empty of anything that could resemble personal belongings, and that's good enough for me.

I dump my bag in the closet, and when I step back out, Andrew's on the bed, his shoes off, his fur jacket open, and his hand reaching into his boy shorts. I swallow my tongue.

"Are you going to join me?" His sexy and raspy tone makes my cock stir, but if I get into bed with him, this will go the exact same way as all my other hookups.

"I … uh … I want to. But aren't you tired? We basically pulled an all-nighter, and not the fun kind with party drugs that keep you up. Maybe we should nap first?"

He looks confused, and I can't blame him.

I need to get out of here. "You rest up. I'm just going to go see if the other guys need any help and maybe check out the place."

"Oh. Okay."

What. Is. Wrong. With. Me?

I turn on my heel and go to leave when Andrew's small voice stops me.

"Seb?"

I glance at him over my shoulder.

"Why am I here?"

I deflate. My head throbs, I'm tired, and I don't want to face this right now, but I need to. I approach the bed and sit on the edge while Andrew sits up. He's so pretty and young.

I'm an idiot. "I might have done something stupid."

"Well, you haven't done me, so that's not true yet. According to your manager anyway."

I wince. "You heard that?"

"It was a small room, and he was kinda yelling, so yeah."

"He's mad at me but not because of you. I'm sure you've seen the news getting around about me. The, uh, photo."

"Why do you think I was so fast to agree to get on a plane with you?" Andrew smiles wickedly, but it falls when he sees this is more serious than that.

"A hookup took that photo without my consent. I didn't even know he'd done it."

"Really? I thought it was a PR stunt."

"It wasn't. And I'm feeling a little ..." *Lost.*

"Violated?" He answers for me. That word works too.

"Thorne told me I need to stop with the cheap tricks and to basically grow up. I wanted to prove to him I could have a real relationship, which is why ..."

Andrew shifts like he's uncomfortable. "Which is why you asked a stripper to come on vacation with you?"

"Told you. Stupid. And now you're here, guilt is eating at me, and it's not right to use you to make a point to someone who's pissed at me."

He starts laughing. "Oh, honey. You know why that man is actually pissed, don't you?"

"Yeah, because I'm making his job ten times harder than it needs to be. It never used to bother me. I mean, we pay him for a reason, but—"

"Oh, you sweet, naïve man. I knew the minute—no, the split second—he saw me on your arm, it was like he wanted to pee on you and mark his territory."

"What do you mean?"

"That man is in love with you."

I huff. "Wow, you could not be more wrong. Thorne is straight."

Andrew blinks at me. "I call bullshit. Did you see his face when you were rubbing my legs in the car and to him it would've looked like you were jerking me off? I swear he was going to push me out of the car and into the snow."

What the fuck is he talking about?

"Trust me on this." He touches my arm. "I know what jealous men act like."

"What do they act like?"

"Neanderthals. You really think his line of questioning on the plane was for his benefit?"

I shake my head. "No, he was doing that to prove to me that I'm the biggest dumbass to ever dumb."

Andrew jumps up and strips out of his coat. "Okay. This is what's going to happen. We're going to nap because you were right about being exhausted. Then this afternoon, I will show you exactly what I mean."

"Wait, you're staying? Even after—"

He climbs under the covers. "I'm not going to lie. I'm disappointed I'm not going to be able to have sex with you, but I'll be happy to stay as a friend and help you."

"Help me what, exactly?"

"Realize I'm right. Then you can do whatever you want with that information."

"Thorne is not in love with me."

He's not. He can't be.

Yet, something inside me hopes for it to be true because spending one night in his arms wasn't enough for me.

I've never, not once, felt as secure as I did the other night with Thorne.

The fantasies of having more of that—of that feeling being a permanent fixture in my life ... I need to know if it's a possibility.

CHAPTER FIVE
THORNE

SEB AND THE stripper disappeared into their room as soon as we arrived, and they haven't come up for air since.

They're not the only ones. Everyone crashed out hard when we arrived, and I'm the only one who's resurfaced to search for coffee.

Maybe that's a good thing. Being alone is what I need to get my head on straight and forget about Seb, the tour, the press … everything. But especially the stripper currently warming Seb's bed.

The large wrought iron clock above a large fireplace in the formal sitting area of this "cabin," aka the ridiculously large mountain chalet, says it's just past lunchtime which means I only got a few hours' sleep. They were restless hours too.

It was nothing like falling asleep with Seb wrapped around me like the other night. I don't think I've ever slept better than when he was in my arms.

I could claim exhaustion from having stayed up the night before trying to squash his photo, but I know it was him. *All him.*

Here, I stupidly thought I could spend this vacation with Seb while the others were all sexed-up. I might not be able to have Seb the way I want him, but I'm always eager for any scraps I can get. Spending these two weeks in the snow with nothing else to do ... I thought we might go skiing, drink by the fire ... I thought we could *talk*. I was looking forward to it.

Now that's crushed by a cute little thing with killer legs and a pretty face.

I find the coffee machine in the kitchen and make myself a cup to take out on the back deck.

There's a firepit and blankets, and I've definitely found the spot I'm going to hole up for the next two weeks. Though, by the time I get the damn thing lit, I almost have to go back inside to defrost.

I wrap myself in a blanket and sit on one of the deck chairs. The warm coffee, the mountain air, and the amazing view of the snowy forest ... mmm, I could get used to this.

"You know how to make a fire?"

I freeze at Seb's voice, refusing to turn to look at him. "I've been known to be useful at some things." *Like running every aspect of your life.*

"Man make fire," the purring Lemon says. "That's sexy."

Don't look, Thorne. Don't look.

I turn.

Damn it.

Lemon's tucked under Seb's arm, wearing Seb's sweats, which are way too long for him, and that ridiculous jacket he came here with. I hate that the image of them together hurts so much.

I've put a lot of shit aside over the last few years because Seb has deserved to be young and free and do what he wants, but hearing him say he wants what Cash and Locke has, it changes everything for me.

It makes me want to march over there, pull Lemon by his stupid bleached hair and throw him out of the house. Because jealous Thorne is clearly rational.

I want to beg Seb to give me a chance. Fuck the consequences and possibly losing the best job I've ever had. To me, he's worth it.

But a huge part of me is sure that when he fails at this, Seb will go back to being his usual no-relationship self.

"There's a pot of coffee in the kitchen," I say and turn back to the fire.

"I'll get you a cup, *babe*."

God, I can hear how happy Lemon's footsteps are from here. They're all bouncy and quick.

Keep your eyes on the fire, Thorne.

I try, but the minute Seb steps into my line of sight, my eyes are on his. He looks exhausted, like he and Lemon didn't get any sleep at all. That thought is what breaks my gaze. I don't need to be thinking about that.

Yet, I still track his movements. He covers himself with a blanket but squirms like he can't get comfortable. "What is ..." He pulls out shining silver material.

I can't help looking at what's in his hand and immediately wish I didn't. Seb's holding Lemon's boy shorts he was wearing earlier.

"Oh, shit." He's quick to pull them under his blanket, but then his eyes are on me. And they don't leave.

He studies me with a heated and assessing gaze. Like he's waiting for my reaction.

I need it to stop before I say something stupid. "Bored of your stripper yet?"

I guess that's better than *"I'm in love with you, you idiot."*

"Why do you want to know?"

"Wondering how long it will be before you ask me to drop him off at the airport."

"Is that all it is?"

No. I *want* to drop him off in the middle of nowhere, but murder is bad. "What else would there be?"

He shrugs. "Dunno."

The door to the house slides open. Oh, good, Lemon is back. At least he's not alone. Cash and Locke follow him out with their own coffees. Yay, fifth wheel time.

Even though there are more than enough seats out here, Lemon puts their drinks on a table next to Seb and lifts the blanket to sit on his lap.

"Oops." He lifts the shorts into the air. "How did these get down here?"

I grit my teeth. God, can I go drop *myself* in the middle of nowhere?

I sip my coffee and try to remain my stoic self.

"So, how were everyone's 'naps'?" Lemon asks. "Our 'nap' was so good, I can barely walk."

Seb groans and buries his head on Lemon's shoulder.

Cash gasps. "We didn't even think about having sex. We *actually* napped. And now I'm depressed because that means we're already that old married couple who would rather sleep than have sex." He stands. "We have to rectify this immediately."

"Please don't," Seb and I say at the same time and share a smile that quickly fades when I look away as fast as possible.

Cash rolls his eyes. "Not here. Inside."

Locke doesn't stir from his spot. "Baby, we have the rest of our lives to have all the sex. I want to drink coffee in front of a fire and relax. You deserve a real vacation."

Cash practically melts back onto his chair.

"Aww," Lemon says and turns to Seb. "I can't wait until we get like that. To be so secure in our relationship that sex isn't the only thing that matters. Until then, I promise to blow you as often and as many times as my mouth can take it."

It's my turn to stand. "And I'm out. I'm gonna take a walk."

"In the snow?" Cash asks.

"Yep." I need to get away from here.

I run to my room for warmer clothes and my boots. There's no direction in mind, though up here, there's really only one road in and out of this place.

I'm out the door in a hurry because I didn't realize a mansion in the Montana hills could be so fucking small and claustrophobia inducing.

Instead of heading back toward the front gate, I go the opposite way, wondering where else the road leads. The gate closes us off from the rest of the world, so I assume I'm heading for a dead end.

I don't care. I just don't want to be in that house.

More snow must have fallen while we were asleep because the road is covered in a thin layer of frost. The sun is high in the sky now, and even though my nose is freezing, the rest of me warms up fast.

The road slopes down around a bend and away from the mansion, and as I keep going, I get a view of a valley and where the road leads to Lone Mountain. Just the thought of Seb and Lemon back there doing all the things I've fantasized about makes my feet move faster.

I don't know how far I've walked until I come across more houses.

These are ten times smaller than the place we're staying, but I think, technically, I'm still on the same property. Maybe.

That's when I realize my feet are wet and numb inside my boots, and as I turn and look back from the direction I came, I can no longer see the house. I turn in a circle and wonder where the fuck I am.

There's only one road, so it's not like I can get lost. I take out my phone, but there's no cell reception.

The door to one of the houses opens, and out steps a massive guy in flannel onto the porch.

The sexiest kind of lumberjack porn runs through my head, and I wonder if I've either slipped on the ice and hit my head and now I'm imagining things, or if I've wandered onto a porn set in the middle of Montana. If this guy asks me to come inside to warm up, I'm going to assume it's the latter.

He's got insanely muscular arms and a thick black beard. He has a bit of a belly, but I can't tell if it's muscular or padding. He's got big thick legs, and his dark hair is tied back.

"You lost?"

Damn, his voice is sexy too. Something familiar about him makes me cock my head, but again, I'm probably thinking of porn.

He studies me. "You got hypothermia?"

I shake my thoughts free. "Sorry, no. I, uh, I don't think I'm lost. Me and my friends are kind of staying up the road."

"Kind of? The way I heard it was people were coming to stay in my house whether I liked it or not and I could either join you or fuck off. I chose to stay away, but you still found me."

That doesn't make any sense. Cash said he blackmailed —*Holy shit.*

My eyes widen.

"Mason? Mason Nash?"

How is this possible? He looks nothing like Mason from Eleven, except around the eyes. It's definitely his eyes.

He folds his arms across his chest. "I haven't changed that much, have I?"

Is he kidding me?

"You've definitely … matured." It was only a few years ago this guy looked like every other pretty boy in a boy band.

Now he's *all man.*

He tilts his head toward the small cottage. "Come inside and warm up. I can drop you back at the house once I'm sure you don't have frostbite."

This definitely feels like the porn scenario again. Am I sure I'm not bleeding from a head wound somewhere and this is all a dream? Lumberjack fantasies are running rampant, but even as I think that, I know if the opportunity came up, I wouldn't take it.

Apart from Mason Nash being straight, so the point's moot anyway, I'm too far gone for Seb for it to be enjoyable. Even if he's back at the house not even giving me a second thought.

The warmth of inside hits me as soon as I step into the small house. It's kept well, but it's old and more the type of place I thought we'd be staying in when you hear the words *cabin in the middle of the woods.*

It's quaint but cozy.

"You can take your shoes and socks off and dry them out by the fire." Mason points to the living room.

"Thanks." I do as he says and also take off my jacket,

gloves, and beanie, and then meet him in the kitchen. "I'm Thorne, by the way. I don't know if you remember me."

"I remember. Thorne Young. Cash Me Outside's manager." Mason rummages in the cupboards, looking for something he can't seem to find.

"What are you doing all the way out here?" I ask.

"This is my mom's house. The land has been in my family for generations, and it used to be a tree farm."

"Ah. That explains the …" I gesture to my face.

"The?"

"The beard. And the flannel. You've got this whole lumbersexual thing going on."

Mason snorts. "Thanks."

"Seriously, man. What happened? Why are you …" I wave around the small cabin. "Here?"

"Uh, because a stupid rock band has taken over my residence? I built that place for my mom and sister and her family to all live with me. They were all 'We love you, but we're good. Thanks.'"

"You live up there all by yourself?"

Mason finally finds what he was looking for and pulls down some hot cocoa. "Drink?"

"Please."

He's silent while he makes it, but if he thinks I'm letting this go, he'd be wrong. I can't help staring at his face. Underneath the tired-looking mountain man is a Hollywood A-lister somewhere, but I'm struggling to see it.

"I actually meant why are you in Montana instead of in LA where you belong," I say when he hands me my cup.

"The world wanted to forget about me, so I let them."

"I'm sure that's not true. What about the guys from Eleven?"

The laugh that falls out of him is harsh. "They're the worst ones."

"What happened with you guys? I know the stories are all bullshit. There was no huge fight, but *something* happened for you to have disappeared like this."

"Why are you walking through the woods trying to kill yourself? Do you know how easy it would've been for you to get lost up here?"

Nice deflection, Mason.

"I was following the road. I was fine."

"Do you know you've walked three miles?"

I lift my drink to take a sip, but I pause halfway to my mouth. "Wait, what?" It couldn't have been that far.

"Want to tell me again how you're fine?"

I slump. "I needed out of there. All of them have groupies with them and Cash has his fiancé."

"Ah. I can't imagine a vacation with a bunch of couples would be much fun."

"I can't imagine living up here alone is much fun either."

"I have my family close by. Who do you have?"

No one. That's who. "You?" I joke.

He laughs into his cup of cocoa. "Only for the next hour before I drop you back where you belong and stay out of the band's way."

"You can't hide forever."

His eyes narrow. "Do you really think Hollywood will welcome me back with open arms? Look at me. I'm not exactly the epitome of Hollywood glamor anymore."

"Word has it, the other boys from Eleven are trying to get you all back together."

He scoffs. "Fuck that. Where were they when my solo career tanked? Where were they when I reached out to them?

Do you know Denver hasn't accepted any of my calls since the last night we were on tour? None of them get to pick and choose when our friendship is convenient for *them*."

Okay, maybe I was wrong about there being no drama over the band breaking up. "I'm sure they still care about you. You can't work with people for as long as you did and not have a special bond. You may drift apart and go your separate ways, but they'll always be your band. I have clients I used to manage, and each and every one of them are important to me. You should see what Harley and the others have to say."

The friendliness disappears completely now, and I'm half expecting him to throw me back outside in the cold and tell me to walk barefoot back to the house. "You going to rat me out to them and tell them where I am?"

"After you saved me from hypothermia and death? No, I think I owe you one."

"Good. Because I'm going to hold you to it."

"I do think you should come up to the house and catch up with Cash and hang out, though. Come have a Hollywood Christmas and maybe get a taste of your old life. It might make you want to go back."

He sips his drink and then wipes milk from his thick beard. "I'll think about it."

Everything about him has changed, and it's a mind trip.

I almost don't want to keep my promise and call Harley Valentine right now because there's something sad behind Mason's eyes that worries me. I guess it's lucky there's no cell reception here or I'd have one angry ex-boy bander on my hands.

Mason hiding away all these years is scary. Not for him, but for me. Mason's hiding from what exactly? Heartbreak? Did someone hurt him or is it really over his career? He seems bitter toward the boys from Eleven, and I know for a fact they used to be really good friends.

Mason eyes me over his cocoa mug. "So, how long have you been in love with Seb?"

I choke on my spit. "What?"

"Or is it Cash? I figured he's been engaged a while now, and you're still their manager, so my power of deduction says it's Seb."

"Why do I have to be in love with anyone?"

"Because I don't know of any man who'd walk three miles in the freezing cold to get away from happy couples if he wasn't in love with someone in that house. As far as I know, the only queer guys in the band are Cash and Seb. I mean, I guess you could be in love with a straight guy, but I'm getting an unresolved feelings vibe not an unrequited thing going on."

I shift uncomfortably in my seat. "I don't think I like this conversation anymore."

Mason smiles, and finally, I see the Mason the world knows.

"You did just show your hand though," I point out.

"How?"

"You're keeping up to date with Hollywood gossip which means you miss it."

Mason shakes his head. "Doesn't mean I belong there. I'm not going back."

Whatever he's holding on to, I hope he finds a way to make peace with it.

Is this what happens when you let emotions fester?

I could give Seb everything he wants, but once my feelings are out there, there's no taking them back. If he's truly ready for something real, I should be the one he turns to.

I'm not entirely convinced he is ready, but if I keep my

mouth shut like I have for the last couple of years, there's no way in hell he'll ever see that he could have it. *With me.*

I don't care if it ruins my career. I need him to know what's inside my heart or I might end up right where Mason is.

Bitter. Alone. And living in the middle of nowhere hoping the world will forget me.

I need to figure out how to put myself out there and tell him, but this trip is definitely not the time to do it. Not while he's here with someone else.

"WHERE IS HE?" I growl.

I've been standing by the front window for an hour, freaking out that Thorne isn't coming back.

Both rented cars are still in the drive, and it's below freezing out there.

"What's going on?" Jasper yawns as he comes down the stairs from his fuckfest and nap.

"Thorne went for a walk," Cash says from where he's been watching me on the couch in front of the fireplace. Locke is using Cash's lap as a pillow while he reads a book, and neither of them care Thorne could be dead for all we know.

"In the snow?" Jasper asks.

"Two hours ago," I point out. "He's probably frozen out there. Literally. Or lost. When he said he was going for a walk, I thought he'd be back in fifteen minutes. Who goes out into the snow for this long?"

"He's a grown-ass adult," Jasper says. "Why do you care?"

Why *do* I care?

"Because your manager is totally in love with your lead

guitarist," Andrew says from his spot on the single armchair. "And I'm totally convinced it's reciprocated."

"It's not," I grunt and go back to watching outside and hoping for a miracle that Thorne will appear.

Andrew doesn't know what he's talking about.

Thorne's a good manager, and he knows how to deal with the band's shit. Just because I have a fuzzy warm sensation toward him doesn't mean I have actual *feelings*. I'm probably projecting daddy issues on him because he takes care of us.

That's his fault for being a decent guy.

"Seb's feeling guilty for letting him storm off in a jealous rage," Andrew says.

Why did I bring him here again? I don't like that he's so … *right*.

I want to dismiss the worry in my gut for exactly that— guilt over Thorne disappearing—but there's a voice screaming in the back of my head yelling that it's so much more than that.

I don't know why this recent scandal has me looking at him differently.

Because he stayed in my bed and held me?

There has to be some sort of psychological explanation for it. Like I'm holding on to the sense of security he brought me and building it into something it's not.

Then I think about where he is now, what he's doing out there in the cold, and I can't help but worry I could lose him. And that thought? The idea of him not being in my life hurts way more than anything else I've ever experienced.

I know *that* means something.

What if he's lost? What if he fell and sprained an ankle and can't get back?

"Thorne is not in love with Seb," Cash says. "Thorne's straight."

Andrew scoffs. "You're as oblivious as Seb."

Cash purses his lips. "He *was* in your bed the other morning."

I tear my gaze away from the blinding whiteness of outside. "Because he crashed out after doing damage control. Nothing happened."

Locke sits up. "Uh, I have to side with Lemon on this one. I see the way he looks at you when you're onstage. I stand by him at nearly every show. Trust me. He's either in love with you or your guitar, and I doubt someone as put together as Thorne would have a thing for inanimate objects."

I look at my best friend for answers. "It can't be true, can it?"

I want it to be. More than I thought I would. But ... I still can't accept that it's real because I can't allow myself to contemplate the possibility. It's a risk my heart might not be able to take.

What if I'm so desperate for what Cash and Locke have that the idea of Thorne being in love with me is appealing because I know him, I like him, and he's *there*.

Well, actually, no, he's not there. He's outside in the fucking cold.

"Told you," Andrew sings. "Totally reciprocated."

"This isn't a face of love." I scowl. "This is the face of worry because he's been outside for way too long, and I don't want him to die."

"Because you love him." Andrew lifts his chin. Smug bastard.

"Shut up. *You* love him." My argument makes no sense, but I don't care.

Cash bursts out laughing. "I think the stripper is right."

I throw up my hands. "Fuck this. If none of you are going to worry about him, I'll go find him. Where are the car keys?"

"Do you even know how to drive in snow?" Cash asks.

"It can't be that hard."

I have to do *something*.

I search through the drawers of the small table in the foyer, but they're empty. The coat closet is next. Frantically, I search through the coats on the rack, looking for Jasper's or Greg's, whoever drove the other car because Thorne has his on him.

Maybe he has the keys.

"Damn it!" Now I'm just throwing the coats everywhere.

"Seb." Cash's calm voice comes from right behind me.

"I need the keys," I say.

"Seb," Cash says again and gently grabs my arm.

"What?" I spin to face him, and my chest rises and falls heavier than it should be.

I think I'm hyperventilating.

Cash's eyes are sympathetic as he tilts his head. "Oh." His voice is soft. "He is right, isn't he? You have feelings for Thorne."

"I don't fucking know. But I do know he could be out there injured or fucking dead, and none of you are doing anything to help me find him." Shit, tears fill my eyes. I try to blink them away but only more come.

And fuck.

Fucking fuck fuck.

I think I'm in love with Thorne.

I don't know what to do with that.

"I can't lose him," I whisper.

"We'll find him." Cash is using his soothing voice—the one he uses when I get agitated by overeager fans thinking they're welcome to our bodies without permission.

Cash handles the ass grabs and cock groping a hell of a lot better than I do, and he knows how to calm me down from making a scene.

The sound of a car pulling up outside reaches my ears, and my heart skips a beat.

I don't even hesitate to rush outside. I'm preparing for the worst, like a patrol car coming to tell us they found a body or something as equally dramatic.

But no.

There's Thorne, all blond and gorgeous stepping out of some random guy's truck.

My chest fills with relief, and I want to run to him, throw my arms around him and hold him.

Then I see that he's *smiling*, and all those good feelings about his return die. It's freezing out here, and I don't have shoes on, only socks. My long T-shirt does shit all to protect me from the cold, but all I feel is red, hot anger.

He gets closer, that carefree smile still on his face, and what the actual fuck?

I shove him. "Where were you? We were worried sick." My voice cracks.

"Correction," Cash says from the doorway. "Seb was worried sick."

Thorne blinks at me, and his smile fades. "You were worried about me?"

"You've been gone for two hours! In this cold …" I let out a loud breath. "Where were you? Who dropped you off?"

"A friend."

"We're in the middle of Montana, and you made a friend?"

Thorne's gaze darts behind me. "You made a friend and brought him along. Maybe you should be more worried about what he's doing."

I'm trying to decipher the look in his eyes as he flicks his attention back to me. His chin juts out in a defiant way, and he's pulling that face he always does when he doesn't want to give anything away.

I can't get a good read on him. I've never been able to.

I try to search past his distracting blue eyes to see if what Andrew is saying could be real. If Thorne has any romantic feelings toward me at all. There's nothing.

"You're right." I step back. "I should be worried about what he's doing instead of you. Because that's the way it works. I can't be worried about my manager wandering off in the damn snow and disappearing just because I'm here with someone. You're absolutely right." I shiver, but I don't know if it's from my wet feet or from frustration.

"Let's get you inside and out of the cold." Thorne tries to take hold of my arm, but I pull away.

"Just, don't disappear again." I barrel past everyone watching and back into the house.

Only, now I don't know where to go.

This whole storming off thing isn't as effective if you don't know which direction you're going.

"Seb, wait," Thorne says.

I turn and try to keep the flood of emotions from showing. Relief, anger, confusion … love? I don't know what I'm feeling right now.

"I'm sorry," he says. "I didn't know you were worried about me or I would've had Mason call the house."

"I knew it!" yells Andrew from behind us. "Can I go stalk him? Where is he? Oh my God, this is so cool. I'm staying in Mason Nash's house?" He squees.

Thorne winces. "Now might be a good time to bring up the NDA with him."

"Definitely."

Especially with all the crap he's spewing about Thorne and I having a thing for each other.

"Make it happen." I storm away and head for Lemon's and my room while Thorne deals with the awkward parts of fame.

As soon as I cross the threshold and close the door behind me, tears sting my eyes, and I don't understand why.

Adrenaline flows through me, left over anger from Thorne worrying me half to death by disappearing and then turning up as if nothing was wrong.

And what the fuck is up with that shit about him not realizing I'd care? Of course I fucking care.

I pace the room, my feet still cold from running out in the snow in just my socks. Ugh, my socks. I reach down and get rid of them, flinging them wherever.

I'm so keyed up. I want to keep yelling at Thorne. I want him to see ...

See what?

I want him to see that I'm not just his client. I never have been. Maybe in the beginning, but since then we've grown close. And okay, sure, I can see why Lemon would think it was more than it is, but if Thorne can't even admit to being my friend, what in the world makes Lemon think he'd be *in love with me*?

Then I think about what Locke said—how Thorne watches me from the side of the stage. I think about all the times Thorne has called me his client. It's always when I've shown him any kind of affection. As if he needs the words to keep that barrier between us.

Or am I now reading into *everything*?

I wish I had some fucking answers.

The memory of waking up next to him the other morning reminds me of my exact thoughts.

Thorne would make the perfect partner—you know, if he wasn't straight.

Did gay Christmas elves sprinkle gay fairy dust to make my ideal guy a reality?

This train of thought is dangerous because if Lemon's wrong, and I've already built this all up in my head, finding out Thorne isn't in love with me won't only disappoint me, it will crush my soul.

Does that mean what I think it means?

Is Lemon right?

I need to find out.

I TELL myself not to read into Seb's reaction to me being gone. He was being considerate and nothing else. But as he runs upstairs to his and Lemon's room, I can't help noticing how everyone is staring at me now, as if waiting for me to say something. What, I don't know.

"Lemon?" I say as politely as I can. "We have business we need to discuss."

"I bet we do." Lemon prances, yes fucking prances, toward me.

"Dining room. I'll go get the laptop."

It's been a while since we've had to ask someone to sign an NDA, but as soon as Seb asked for one last night, I emailed the label's lawyers.

As I get the laptop and go back to the kitchen alcove where there's a large twelve-seater cedar dining table, Lemon blinks up at me with an innocent yet somehow condescending smile on his face.

He bounces in his seat. "Is this where you tell me to stay away from your lead guitarist and put me on a flight home?"

I wish.

"Nope. I'm here to get you to sign a nondisclosure agreement. It basically says you can't repeat anything that happens on this trip to anyone. Especially the media."

"Pfft. Like anyone will believe me anyway."

"That's not really the point. I'm trying to ensure you're not going to make a quick buck out of Seb like the last guy."

"I'm not here for a quick buck, but I'll take something that rhymes with that." The little smartass smirks.

"That's yours and Seb's business. I don't need to know."

He clasps his hands together. "You mean you don't want to know."

I grit my teeth. "Read over this and sign it when you're done." I turn the laptop over to him.

Lemon settles back in his seat and folds his arms. "And if I don't?"

"Then this is where I tell you to stay away from my lead guitarist and put you on a flight home."

He leans forward, skims the document, and then uses his finger to scribble an electronic signature. "Done."

I take it back and email it off to the lawyers. "You can go now."

"What if I don't want to?"

"Don't want to what?"

"What if I want to stay here and talk to you?"

"I'd say your time with Seb is short, and if I were you, I'd make the most of being with him instead of being in here talking to a no one."

Lemon stands and makes his way around the table to my side and leans his hip against the wood. "You're not a no one to Seb."

I scoot my chair away to put a bit of space between us.

"That doesn't mean we need to bond or some shit. You're temporary. They all are."

Lemon frowns. "How can he not see how in love with him you are?"

"*Excuse me*?"

He stands upright. "You're completely in love with him. It's obvious. Well, to everyone else except him. And Cash. But if Cash paid attention, he'd see it too."

"I have no idea what you're talking about." I take my laptop and hurry to leave the room, but Lemon's voice follows me.

"You can't run away from your feelings forever!"

He's right about that, but I'm not going to pour my heart out in front of everyone where there's no escape when it inevitably blows up in all our faces.

I make my way back into the living room and am met with a billion stares in my direction.

Greg and his hookup have resurfaced. Jasper's girl is by his side. With Cash and Locke all cuddly on the couch, the couples are easy to bypass.

My gaze gets stuck on Seb who's staring at me with an intensity I've never seen directed at me.

For a moment, my heart stutters, and fear cuts through me. That annoying twink better not have been blurting his ridiculously true theory to anyone who will listen.

"What?" I ask.

"Nothing." Cash jumps up from the couch. "Locke and I will take dinner duty tonight."

"Do you even know how to cook?" I ask.

"Hey, you forget I was a struggling musician for years. I know my way around a kitchen."

"Yes, but I was hoping for more than ramen."

Locke stands. "Don't worry. I've got it."

"How long until dinner?" Jasper asks.

"When it's ready!" Cash yells back.

Seconds later, both Jasper and Greg disappear back upstairs with their women. I get the feeling we'll barely see those four all vacation, and I'm totally okay with that.

That leaves Seb and me.

Oh, and Lemon.

"What did I miss?" that bouncy, annoying voice asks as he bounds into the room.

"Cash and Locke are cooking dinner, and the others are … busy," I say and don't take my eyes off Seb.

He's still staring at me, and I have no doubt Lemon has been running his mouth.

"I'm going to go back outside and relight the fire." I need to get out of here. Though after my excursion today, I know not to leave the house.

When Mason was driving me back, I couldn't believe how far I'd walked.

Anything could've happened. If it had started snowing and the road got completely covered in white, I could've actually gotten lost.

But it's impossible to be in the same room as Seb and Lemon without getting irrationally jealous, so I need to do something.

I throw my warmer jacket back on, as well as my beanie, gloves, and scarf, and head out to the fire pit.

The sun is starting to set, and it's going to be even colder soon.

The fire from earlier is nothing but charred wood, and I realize I should've told the guys to try to keep the fire going so we didn't lose it. Now I have to start all over again.

I get more firewood from the pile Mason left for us and arrange them in a peak with kindling underneath. It takes a few tries to get the actual wood lit for it to burn properly, but then it ignites, and I'm happy I don't have to give up and go back inside where they are. I guess I could hide in my room if it comes down to it.

I stand by the fire and wrap myself in one of the blankets, watching the sky turn a billion different colors as the sun slowly disappears.

The loneliness tries to overwhelm me, but I push it back down.

I've been out here for maybe half an hour when I hear the door behind me click open, and I freeze. I don't need to turn to know who it is, and I really, really, really don't want to do this.

Seb appears at my side, and no matter how many times I tell myself to keep staring at the flickering flames as the fire grows, I know it's impossible. My gaze gravitates to him like it always does.

His eyes are weary, and he looks exhausted. "So Andrew has this crazy theory."

So he has been running his mouth.

"I heard. Your boy toy is obviously on drugs. Lots and lots of them."

Seb huffs, and a puff of steam comes out his mouth. "I thought so too."

I turn back to the fire. "Glad we cleared that up. Good talk. You can go back inside now."

Please, please, please stop torturing me like this. I want to tell him everything. I want to break down and confess how much I've been in love with him these last couple of years, but I can't. I'm not ready to put everything on the line. Maybe after the tour I can take a step back and ask for time off to decide what I want to do and how I want to do it. The band needs to be in a position to find a new manager without having to worry about completing show dates on a tight schedule with no one to make sure they're where they're supposed to be and when.

"Yeah, I'm not going back inside," Seb says. "I realized something today."

"What's that?"

He moves in closer, and I find myself holding my breath.

"I want him to be right," Seb whispers.

My heart stutters.

I swallow hard.

I can't look at him as I ask, "What, so you can mock me about it?"

He ignores my accusation and keeps talking. "At first I thought he was crazy."

I scoff. "Insane."

"But things like that. Right there."

Finally, I turn to him. "What things?"

"Your go-to defense mechanism when you want to put distance between us. You do this thing where you emphasize a point like you want to believe what you're saying. You get this look in your eye like you're scared I'll figure out the truth. Every time there's a scandal about us in the tabloids, you act like you are right now. And you've been looking at me like that ever since I turned up with a stripper. I thought it was a media problem, but now ..."

I'm always so good at hiding my feelings—or I thought so —but the fact he can read me when I don't want him to makes me edgy.

I'm scared he can see everything. How much I pine for

him. Ache for his touch. The amount of times I've imagined what his mouth tastes like and what it would feel like to sink inside his body.

"I ..." My lips close together. Then open. I don't know what to say. I don't know what I *can* say.

Seb nods. "Yep. That's what I thought. And now I'm taking a risk. A big fucking risk, because, Thorne?"

"Mm?"

"I want to be right about this so damn bad."

He is. About *everything*.

"Seb—"

He moves closer, sucking all the air out from the entire state of Montana. Then his strong mouth is on mine, and all I can do is let it happen because I am not in control right now. Nowhere near it. My brain screams at me to stop it, but my heart is screaming louder to seize this moment. It might be the only moment we get.

Seb's tongue parts my lips, and as I open for him, he groans and pulls me against him.

Seb is kissing me.

Sebastian Rose is kissing Thorne Young.

Nope. There is no way this is happening.

There are too many layers of clothing. Too much bulk surrounding us. I want to put my hands inside his jacket and run my hands over the chest and abs I watch onstage. I want my mouth to explore more than just his tongue and the scruff around his lips. I need to feel the rough scrape of his beard all over me. But I also need to stop this.

I need to stop the shooting sparks of lust coursing through me.

I need ... fuck, I need Seb. More than I ever have before.

He smells like smoke but tastes like *forever*.

And holy fuck does he know how to kiss.

Shit, what are we doing?

He moans into my mouth, and I realize I don't care what we're doing, what we're screwing up, or what an awkward *you're fired* conversation will come afterward, I don't want him to stop.

But I *have* to.

I pull away but can't bring myself to let go of him. "You're here with someone else."

"Not anymore. I told him he needs to go home."

My eyes widen. "You did what?"

"I want *you*. I went searching for my perfect man in the wrong place, but Lemon wasn't a complete waste. He made me realize what I have right in front of me."

I want to believe him. More than anything, I want the words spewing from his mouth to be the truth, but I'm scared he only likes the idea of me.

"We should think about this," I say.

"I don't need to. I know what I want."

I force myself to step away from him. "And since when have you known? When we got on a plane less than twenty-four hours ago, you said you wanted to make it work with a stripper."

"That was before."

"Before what?" The edge in my voice gives away how much I don't want to fight this. I want to give myself over to him more than anything, but not at the expense of my heart and my career.

"Before I knew you were even a possibility. How long?"

"How long, what?"

"Have you been into guys?"

I fold my arms across my chest. "I'm bi. Always have been. It's what made me fight to become your manager. I knew you and Cash were out, and I wanted to represent you guys so there wouldn't be any queer erasure going on."

"And you didn't think you should tell *us* that?"

I avert my gaze because keeping it a secret has been hard, but it's also been a necessity. "I didn't want any complications …"

"Meaning?"

"I didn't want the possibility of either you or Cash getting bored on tour and messing with me. My job is important, and I wouldn't piss it away for a quick fuck with a client."

Seb inches closer, closing the gap I'm trying to keep between us. "And if I kissed you again, what would that be? Would that classify as messing with you?"

I lick my lips, still tasting him there, and at this point, I don't care if he's messing with me because I want to kiss him again.

"It depends," I hedge. "Are you kissing me for the right reasons?"

"What are the right reasons?"

"That you want me for more than a fuck. That you're willing to put my job, the band's reputation, and everything on the line for it? Because that's what you'll be doing. This thing between us, it can't be temporary, and it can't be an experiment to see if you can hold a relationship. I can't be what you wanted Lemon to be. It needs to be *real*."

Seb hesitates. "That's a lot of pressure."

"I know it is. But this isn't one of those times where you can act now and deal with the consequences later."

"I *know* that."

"All I need is for you to want me because I'm *me*. Not because I'm convenient."

He lets out a harsh laugh. "My feelings for you are anything but convenient."

"What's that supposed to mean?"

"If I wanted an easy fuck, I wouldn't have told Andrew to go home."

"Being with him would be less complicated," I point out.

Seb closes the gap between us. "Since when have you ever known me to take the easy road?"

"I don't want to make your life messier than it already is."

"When you disappeared today, I've never been so scared in my entire life," he whispers. "I thought I could lose you and that's when I realized Andrew was right."

"About what?"

Seb's thumb traces over my jaw. "I'm in love with you as much as you are with me. I just ... I didn't know that's what it was until it was pointed out. Casual admiration and complete trust doesn't exactly scream bone-deep forever type of love, but it's definitely a great basis for it. If I'd known there was a possibility for more, maybe I would've seen it sooner for what it really is."

"What is it?"

"The type of love that slaps you in the face."

My lips part as I suck in a stilted breath. "Getting involved isn't smart. It's why—"

"It's why you never told me how you felt?"

I nod. "The media will love it, the label will hate it, and Cash and the guys, they'll worry about what it means for the band."

"I know all of that. I just don't care."

"If I kiss you again, that's it," I say, my voice a low rasp.

"Lines have been crossed, and I need to know you're ready for it."

He matches my tone. "I'm so ready for it."

My eyes flutter closed, and I finally let myself give in to it. "That's all I need."

THORNE TOUCHES his lips to mine this time. He kisses me. And the minute his mouth lands on me, it's as if something unleashes, and it happens all at once. The explosion of emotions I've been suppressing for what feels like years.

Every smile he has sent my way from the side of the stage. Every fight we've had over the clothes Cash and I wear to the shit we say in interviews. He's always had this eye-rolling yet proud expression.

The random affection bouncing around in my chest about him is new, but his constant presence in my life makes it easier to accept.

I understand Thorne's hesitance about doing this. The timing for this has been weird, but without a doubt, the warmth and fullness inside me when I'm around Thorne is more than a manager and client relationship. It's more than just *friends*.

Just like this kiss is not soft or caring, yet it's everything. It's *claiming*, and my soul responds to that. It responds in ways it never has to another person. Kissing is all mouths and tongue, but with Thorne? It's a fucking life experience. Butter-flies warm my gut, and my skin feels like it's on fire.

The most unexpected thing about this all is that when his tongue pushes into my mouth, I not only melt into him but I one hundred percent let him take charge.

I let his hands roam over my back and grip my ass. I let his tongue take control of mine, and with every stroke, I submit more and more.

That's not my usual MO when it comes to sex. And I really fucking hope that's where this is leading.

Under other circumstances, I'm the one to take control because I need to. Because if I didn't, shit would be spread about me in the tabloids. I've never been able to trust anyone I've been with, but with Thorne, I'm able to let that all go.

His kisses are hard, his grip on my hips even harder, and the more he pushes, the more I relax, and the more control I give to him.

"We need to go inside," he murmurs against my lips.

Yes. Inside. Bed.

"You go first," Thorne says. "Go to my room and take off all your clothes. I'll be in there in a couple of minutes."

"You don't want the others to know?"

"Not yet. And especially not now."

Oh. Right. That's not going to be a fun conversation.

Thorne nods in the direction of the house. "Go."

I'm quick to obey, but as soon as I enter the doors, Andrew blinks up at me from the couch in the formal sitting area.

"Weren't you …" *Leaving? Rude much, asshole?*

He smiles. "Going home? I am. Apparently Greg's woman isn't too happy with him. He's going to drop us both off at the airport. There's one last flight tonight."

"Oh. Umm, cool." I shove my hands in my pockets.

"You don't need to babysit me. I'm a big boy."

I relax. "Thank you. You're the best."

"I know I am. Just call me Cupid. Go get that man of yours."

I scramble to do just that. I head down the hall to where Thorne's room is.

Anticipation swirls in my gut. I can't wait to be naked with him. I want skin on skin and for him to hold me close like he did the other night but with added sex.

The nerves start to kick in when I get down to my boxer briefs.

This is all so new, but in a weird way, it feels like it's been a long time coming.

When he steps through the door, he eyes me from head to toe, and his gaze fills with pure lust.

"You're not naked."

My usual quip to an obvious statement dies on my tongue. "Neither are you."

"Undress me," he orders.

I peel off his jacket, and he helps me get rid of his sweater and shirt. His wide chest is smattered with light blond hairs.

Damn.

I run my hands over his muscles.

"Pants." His commanding voice goes straight to my cock.

That's new.

I've always liked the way he handles us in the band. He's no bullshit and tells us when we're out of line or being spoiled brats. He tells us what we need to do to sell albums. Thorne doesn't ask things of us, he demands. I had no idea in this context his bossiness could be so fucking hot.

I pop the button on his jeans and lower the zipper, then

work them down his thighs. He steps out of them, and now we're both left in our underwear.

Instead of making me take them off, he steps back and does it, slowly lowering his boxers until his hard cock springs free. I'm locked in a trance as he steps forward and hooks his thumbs into the sides of my underwear. He tugs them down my legs until I step out of them, and as he stands again, he wraps his arm around my back and pulls me against him.

I look him right in the eyes and search for any hesitance. All I see is burning lust and a whole lot of love. It can't be the first time he's looked at me like this, but it's definitely the first time I'm taking notice.

"Is this really happening?" I ask.

Thorne lowers his head and sucks on my neck. "It is. And I'm going to show you in every which way I've been fanta-sizing about this."

"Yeah?" I throw my head back, giving him more access as he works his way over my collarbone.

"And it's going to be different than all those groupies you've been with."

"How?"

"I won't let you use my body. You're the one who's going to end up being wrung out. Every hole used until I come."

"Holy shit," I breathe. "I haven't … I mean …"

"I know you haven't bottomed since that asshole the first year you became famous."

That was my first lesson in realizing my bedroom antics weren't just for me and who I was with anymore. This guy wrote an entire blog about his night with Sebastian Rose and then monetized it with ads when it went viral.

"But you're going to bottom for me," Thorne says.

"I kinda love how you're not asking."

"Since when do I ever *ask* you to do something?"

"But … if I didn't want to?"

Thorne pulls back and pierces me with his bright blue eyes. "Then you tell me. I might be bossy, but in my bed, you never have to do something you don't want to."

"I want to." I smile. "I just needed the reassurance I could change my mind."

"Do you trust me?" Thorne asks.

"More than anyone else in this world."

"Good. Then you know I'll stop if you tell me to, and I won't tell a fucking soul what happens between us."

Honestly, that might be the biggest turn on of all. Letting down my walls, letting Thorne in, I know I will never have to hesitate to ask for what I want because he would never exploit it.

"Now I need you on your knees," Thorne rasps.

I immediately sink to the floor. It's surprising how easy I'm giving up control to Thorne, but at the same time, it's not. If I had the choice, I would be the one on my knees, I would be the one bending over, but the past few years haven't allowed me that luxury.

Thorne sits on the edge of the bed and spreads his thighs. His body is long and lean, and I can't help admiring it. I want to run my tongue over every inch.

He gestures for me to come closer, and I shuffle on my knees until I'm in between his legs, but when I run my hands up his calves, he stops me.

He grips my wrists. "No hands. I want only your mouth."

A shiver runs down my spine while my cock jerks.

"Put your hands behind your back."

I immediately do as he says and then blink up at him.

"You're so hot down there." Thorne reaches for me and

fists my long hair in his hand. His grip is tight, and my scalp stings, but fuck, if I don't love it.

My mouth inches closer as he guides me toward his swollen head. His cock is long and thick, and how in the hell did I not know how big his dick is?

I've seen Thorne shirtless countless times but have never had the pleasure of seeing south of the border.

His dick is something to be worshiped and put on display. I make a decision. "I'm buying you sweatpants for Christmas. Tight ones. Then I'm throwing out every pair of underwear you own."

Thorne laughs. "I'm mildly offended you haven't bought me a Christmas present yet."

"Oh, I have, but I just thought of a better one. You can have both."

"I'd trade both of them in for your mouth to stop babbling and start sucking."

Yeah, I'm not going to do that. Not right away. I'm going to draw this out and drive him crazy to the point he won't be able to hold back. I want to break him, see if I can crack that tough exterior of his. I've seen glimpses, but I've never seen him completely let go.

Tentatively, I run my tongue over his leaking cock. He tastes like heaven, and I close my mouth over the head and suck gently.

Thorne moans and writhes.

I roll my tongue as I pull off him again and then lick my way down the underside of his hard shaft. Moving lower, I tease his balls.

Thorne gasps. "Seb ..."

He's trimmed and perfectly manscaped, so I could stay down here all night. I want to use my hands. I want to use every weapon in my arsenal, but I know Thorne will stop me.

When I work my way back up, I suck him into my mouth as far as I can. I can tell he's fighting to push my head down so I can take more of him. He's trying to be polite, but fuck that.

I pull back up, licking, sucking, and teasing just the tip, driving him nuts. It has to be frustrating for him, and as I lift my gaze and look him in the eye, he catches on to what I'm doing.

"Fuck. You're as much a smartass in bed as you are out of it."

"Mm-hmm," I hum.

He loses his fight and forces my head down while he thrusts upward. His cock tickles the back of my throat, and my eyes water, but I love it. His hips lift off the bed, thrusting again, and I tell my gag reflex to relax.

Thorne begins to tremble as he grunts and does it again and again, and then—

There's a knock at the fucking door.

"Hey, uh, guys?" Locke so knows what's going on in here.

Thorne's eyes widen, and he tries to pull out of my mouth, but I suck hard and subtly shake my head.

"What's … uh …"

I bob my head again.

"*Up*?" Thorne scrambles for words, and I smile internally.

"Dinner's ready," Locke says through the door.

"We'll …" Thorne takes a deep breath and lets the next sentence out in a rush. "Be right there."

I shake my head again.

"I mean! No! We'll be out … Soon. Start without us."

"Okay." Locke's footsteps retreat.

"Up," Thorne orders. I want to protest, but then he says, "I need inside you now."

I release him immediately and scramble onto my hands and knees on the bed. My cock hasn't had any attention yet, and it aches with need. I reach for it, but as suspected, Thorne doesn't allow it.

"Hands above your head."

"Come on," I whine but do it.

"Stay like that." Thorne crosses the room and gets supplies, while I squirm impatiently on the bed. My balls tingle, and I'm getting impatient. I want to touch myself. I want Thorne's hands on me.

I just ... *want*.

What is taking Thorne so long? I turn my head as the bed behind me dips, and anticipation surges through me.

Warm lips land on my left ass cheek and then my right. Soft hands run up my sides, then his body covers mine. Light kisses trail along the back of my neck and shoulder blades, while the sound of the lube cap opening echoes around the room.

Thorne's warmth leaves, sending a shiver up my spine as he kneels behind me. Then, simultaneously, a wet finger teases my rim while he reaches under me and pulls my cock toward him, bringing it between my legs. He pushes his finger inside my hole and strokes my cock.

The breathy croak that leaves my lips is muffled when I lower my head and bury it in the pillow below me.

"You look so hot spread out for me like this," Thorne rumbles.

The praise amplifies the sensation on my dick and in my ass.

He adds a second finger, and I grunt, adjusting to the

change. To compensate, he strokes my dick a little harder, and I relax for him.

I turn my head so I can take a deep breath, but I can only suck in short gasps as his fingers hit my prostate.

Then he dips his head. His rough stubble scrapes along my skin while he sucks my balls into his mouth. I shout out so loud, I'm sure everyone in this whole mansion can hear me, but I can't help it.

My ass pulses around his fingers, my dick leaks, and my balls tighten. If he doesn't hurry up and fuck me, this might be all over before he gets inside me.

"Thorne," I breathe. "I need you. Now."

His mouth leaves my sac, and I'm able to pull back from the edge, but his hands don't stop. "Not yet."

His hands move in sync, his fingers hitting my prostate on every upstroke on my cock. It only takes a few seconds for the tension to coil through me once again, sending me way too close to coming early. "I can't … I'm gonna come if you keep going."

"Mm, wouldn't want that." He slows but doesn't stop. He does add a third finger, and the stretching sting helps, but nowhere near enough.

"I'm ready," I plead.

"No, you're not. Not yet."

I groan in protest. Or is it pleasure? I have no idea.

"I never thought this would happen. Ever," he rambles as he keeps finger fucking me. His hand stroking me has slowed, but that doesn't mean anything when my prostate is being massaged within an inch of my sanity. "I love how you are right now—splayed out for me and begging."

"Please put me out of my misery. Please, please, please."

"Are you sure your hole is ready for me? Because I'm not

going to hold back. One day I'll be able to make love to you, but today is not that day."

"Oh God. Fuck me. Please."

"Yeah?"

"I need your dick."

When he finally pulls his fingers from my body, I manage to catch my breath while he puts the condom on. I'm so wrung out already I can't even lift my gaze to look.

The head of his cock presses against my hole, and my eager body pushes back, wanting more. I want to be filled. I want Thorne inside me.

I don't know if I'm cut out to be anyone's boyfriend or partner. A lifetime ago, I'd dated. I had boyfriends while I was a struggling artist, but I can't say I've ever been in love before.

Thorne pushes forward, burying deep inside. "Fuck, you feel good."

I shake my head because my short break wasn't long enough. "I can't … I …"

He thrusts again.

"I can't hold out."

"Good. I want you to come. Then I'm going to use your body and drive into you over and over again until you're crying out in pleasure and pain."

I fist the pillow in my hands and grit my teeth.

Thorne follows through on his promise. It only takes two brushes of my prostate to have me crying out and coming completely hands free. I don't think that's ever happened before. My memory fails me because my brain is in my balls.

My cock jerks, and spurts of cum land beneath me.

I want to sink into the mattress. My trembling limbs want to collapse, but Thorne won't let me. He grips my hips hard and starts a punishing pace. He does as he says and uses my body.

"You're even tighter than I imagined," he grits out.

I grunt. "You've imagined this?"

He grips my hair tight and pulls my head back while he blankets me with his body. "Oh, I've imagined so many different things about you and my dick."

"Mmm, maybe I should make it my mission to make each and every one of those fantasies come true."

Thorne's movements falter. "Promise?" His voice barely cuts through the fog of bliss.

"Promise."

Just like that, Thorne tenses and lets out a low moan. He thrusts a few more times, drawing out his orgasm, and hitting my oversensitive prostate. I shudder, and we collapse together in a heap of tired muscles.

I can't remember a time I've ever been so happy to be covered in my own jizz.

Eventually, he rolls off me, but I'm too out of it to move. He gets up, and the door clicks open at some point, but I still don't roll over. My whole body aches.

Thorne returns moments later, and he lets out a sigh. "You look so hot like that. I almost don't want to make you get up."

"Why do I have to move?" I complain.

"To clean up."

Oh, right. I probably should do that. "The best I can do is this." I roll onto my back.

Thorne's still naked, and damn, that's a good sight. His wide shoulders and narrow waist. His short and usually styled and neat hair is messy and sticking up at all angles from sweat. He has a wet cloth in his hands.

"How have I never seen you naked before? We've been on tour busses. We've shared hotel rooms."

"I made sure you never saw me like that." He wipes down my chest, my abs, and then the bed beside me. "Fuck, you came a lot."

I smile like it's something to be proud of. "I've had complaints before."

"Why? It's hot."

"You should try swallowing it all."

His blue eyes fill with heat. "Challenge accepted."

"Later. Right now I want cuddles."

His eyebrows rise. "You're a cuddler?"

"Not usually. It's weird asking randoms for a hug after sex. But, I mean, we're doing this properly, right? I want some damn perks."

"I just cleaned up after your perks." Thorne smirks.

That's what he thinks, but it's so not. I can get sex anywhere—maybe not as mind blowing as what we did—but intimacy? I haven't had anything remotely close to that for years.

Thorne drops the cum-soaked towel and climbs back into bed with me, pulling me close. He smells like sex and after-shave, and as he holds me, I'm probably the most settled I've ever been in someone else's arms.

I needed this more than the sex.

THIS ISN'T REAL LIFE. It can't be. Seb's in my arms, we're half cleaned up but still sweaty messes, and I'm tracing circles on Seb's shoulder like we've done this a million times. I'm still not entirely convinced I'm not dreaming.

"Are you ready to face what's out there?" I ask because I'm not sure I am.

"No. We live in this room now." He snuggles in closer.

"Sounds good to me."

"I do need to piss though, and you don't have a bathroom. We should've done this in my room."

"I'm not going to sleep with you in a bed where you've fucked another man." My chest tightens at the thought of what Seb and Lemon got up to.

"I didn't have sex with him," he says quietly.

"Wait, what?" I move and roll onto my side because I need to see his face when he says that again.

"We made out in the club when we met, but as soon as I saw how disappointed you were when we showed up at the airport, it felt … wrong. I don't think I even kissed him the whole time he was here."

"Really?"

Seb traces his finger over my chest. "I hated how you looked at me, and then on the plane I knew I'd made a mistake, but by then, I didn't know how to tell Andrew he needed to go right back home again, so …"

"So you pretended you were sleeping together."

"Hey, that was Andrew's idea. He had this crazy notion you had a thing for me and wanted to prove it."

I snort. "Totally crazy."

"How long …" Seb doesn't finish his question.

"Hmm?"

"Have you felt this way about me?"

I purse my lips. "I've always thought you were hot and charismatic. From the day I met you, the attraction was there for me, but it was just that—a controllable emotion that could easily be squashed by my work ethic."

"When did it change?"

"About two years ago."

Seb sits up. "Two *years*?"

I nod.

"How … how did I never see it?"

I sit up with him. "I never let you see it. I never thought this would even be a possibility. Not like this. I was always careful not to show any interest because I knew how easy it would be for us to fall into bed and have it not mean anything."

"Are you calling me easy?"

I cock my head. "Are you saying you're not?"

Seb laughs. "No."

"I wanted more than that with you. All or nothing."

"I want it all," he whispers. "I promise. I just ... I don't know how."

"You've been in your famous rock star bubble for a few years, so I know to give you some leeway." I lean in and brush my lips against his before forcing myself to pull back. "And I guess we better get back out there and tell them what's going on."

Seb's stomach rumbles. "And get that dinner we skipped."

"That too."

We both climb out of bed, and I watch Seb's naked form as he picks up his clothes from the floor. He looks thoroughly fucked. Which he is. I can't wait to do it again.

I grab a fresh pair of jeans out of my luggage.

"Nuh-uh," Seb says. "Sweatpants."

"You don't think I should look semi-professional to tell my other clients I'm sleeping with their bandmate?"

"No. You should look sexy as fuck so they can see how irresistible you are and forgive me for possibly screwing things up with you professionally."

I drop the jeans and put on the sweats. For him. "Are you worried about the guys' reactions?"

"Nah, they'll be happy for us, but if you're under the impression I won't be threatened about ruining this, you're delusional. You're an amazing manager, and if this doesn't work out, we're all screwed."

Seb's experiencing the exact fear that's held me back from taking this step for so long.

Anything could happen. The media could find out about us and make it a big deal. Seb's usual groupie antics might be too hard for me to handle. If we're doing this for real, I'd need him to promise he wouldn't sleep with any of them, but that's not all there is to it.

Fans always have their hands all over them during meet and greets, asking for kisses, offering hotel room numbers and keys. There's nothing he can really do about that other than smile politely and flirt his way out of it, but I'd be on the sidelines witnessing it. It's always turned my stomach to see, but now that I've had him? It will kill me.

But it's his job, and I will need to deal with it. Just like I will still need to do my job and protect the needs of the band first and foremost.

"Maybe we can make them a promise," I say.

"What kind of promise?"

"If this doesn't work out, we put the band first."

Seb approaches me, fully clothed now. "I don't know if I can promise that."

"No?"

"After that, I don't think we can go back."

"So if this is the biggest mistake of our lives, that's it for us professionally? I have to walk away?"

He hangs his head "Fuck, I don't know." His hair falls in his face, and I reach to tuck it behind his ears. His eyes meet mine. "Maybe we need to make sure this works out then."

"That easy, huh?"

"Hey, I just had sex with Thorne Young. If that can happen, anything is possible." Seb leans in and kisses me, and I don't think I will ever get used to it, but I can guarantee I'm going to take advantage of the possibility every chance I get.

I pull back. "Let's go tell them."

"Ugh. Fine." He takes my hand, and that's how we present ourselves to the guys who we find in the home theater room.

They're watching one of the *Jurassic World* movies, and we step in front of them, blocking their view.

My heart thuds and then skips a beat.

Cash pauses the movie and cocks a very smug eyebrow at us. Hmm, maybe I should be the one to lead this, but … Seb's their friend. I'm just their manager. Maybe it should come from Seb.

"Thorne and I had sex."

God, not like that.

"Locke heard," Cash snickers.

I groan and rub my temples while everyone in the room erupts into laughter.

Seb pats my arm. "Oh, hon, you didn't think I'd be subtle and use tact, did you?"

"I should've known better." I slip into professional mode. "Okay, here's the deal. Seb and I are—"

"Going to have sex again. Lots and lots of sex."

I glare at him, and he holds up his hands in surrender.

"We're together," I say, turning back to the guys. "I know that changes the dynamic between all of us, so we wanted to get any awkward conversations out of the way."

"What happens if you break up?" Jasper asks.

"Way to ease us into it," I say. "We've agreed that we won't let our relationship affect our professional lives."

"Wait, I did?" Seb asks. "I remember promising to never break up so we can avoid awkwardness."

"That sounds like a completely logical and flawless plan," Cash says dryly.

"In all seriousness," I say. "My only priorities are the band and Seb, and luckily, whatever is good for the band should be good for him."

The three band members look around at each other, while Jasper's groupie and Locke watch on in fascination.

"What if we agree as a band for an out clause?" Cash asks.

Seb's brow furrows. "An out clause?"

"I think we can all agree, both of you are important members of the band."

My chest warms. I've always felt a part of these guys, but not in the same way as each of them—not a fully-fledged member of the band. Knowing Cash sees me that way is probably the most fulfilling accomplishment I could achieve as a manager.

"So," Cash continues. "What if you have an out clause where Thorne promises to stay with the band but becomes our direct contact at the label instead of our tour manager? We'd still have your great insight," he says to me and then turns to Seb. "And you won't have to see him every day."

Seb looks like he doesn't like that idea. His face winces like he's tasting something unpleasant. "You're talking contingencies for if I fuck this up, and I don't want to think about that."

I squeeze his hand. "That's not what this is. Cash is being smart. Protecting both you and the future of the band. Anything could happen. Just because I've had this idea of us for years, doesn't mean that when it actually happens it will be all smooth sailing. I will still make you wear the clothes you hate, sing the songs you don't want to. Maybe you'll come to resent me for it now we've crossed that professional line."

My neck burns, and I'm self-conscious as I spout all this shit in front of everyone, but if we're going to be together, a lot of our relationship will be like that. Because being with Seb comes as a package deal.

"That's ... understandable," Seb says. "I still don't like it because I don't want to have to think about contingencies, but it makes sense."

"Then we're happy for you," Cash says, like he speaks for the whole band.

I narrow my gaze. "You guys already talked about this, didn't you?"

"Yep." Cash grins.

See? They're involved whether Seb and I want them to be or not. But I wouldn't have it any other way because they're part of Seb. And now I'm part of them.

Cash stands, and his deep brown eyes cut through me. "You know, it makes sense." He waves a finger between us. "You two."

"It does?" I ask.

"I didn't see it before, but when Locke told me how you've looked at Seb for years without us knowing, I started thinking it over, and I realize you've been pretty obvious and we've all been too lost in our own personal worlds to notice. I like you for Seb. He needs a commanding presence to ground him."

"Hey," Seb whines, but when we look at him, he relents. "Okay, that's fair. But still ... ouch, dude."

"It's not a bad thing," Cash says and steps over to him. "I want you to be happy like I am with Locke, and Thorne can give that to you."

"I think so too," Seb says, his voice low.

His eyes meet mine. When he smiles in a shy and uncertain way that is so not Seb, I can't resist pulling him against me.

He fits against me, and nothing has ever felt so right.

"I promise to give you whatever you need," I whisper into his hair.

"What if I need a—"

"Within reason. I'm talking happiness, support, an emotional rock. Not, like, a unicorn wearing a rainbow harness."

Seb snuggles into my side. "It's like you can really see into my soul." He turns to the others. "Speaking of which, who wants to go shopping with me tomorrow? I need to get Thorne a new Christmas present."

"I'll go," Locke says. "I need something extra for Cash."

Seb smiles. "Perfect."

Apparently my man's soul is full of unicorns and me in sweatpants, and I'm totally okay with that.

THE NEAREST MALL is about an hour away from the mansion, so Locke and I are gone for most of the day. He struggles with something to get Cash who can literally afford to buy anything he wants, and I keep flip-flopping over what to get Thorne. Other than sweatpants one size too small for him. Those were the first stop.

I want something else though. Something that shows I'm all in and that I'm taking our relationship seriously even though it's all new for me and my feelings for Thorne are still … confusing.

It's hard to comprehend how it's hit me all at once, which makes me think about every nice deed he's done for me, all those times I thought of him as more than just our manager. Every time he'd call me a client, and it made me feel sick.

Just how long have I been in love with him and not known? I guess it doesn't matter in the big scheme of things, but it does make choosing this gift difficult.

It doesn't help that the mall is packed with people doing

last-minute shopping, and it's pure chaos as people empty shelves of crap to give their family members.

We walk past a row of ugly Christmas sweaters, and I point at them.

"No," Locke says emphatically.

"I was actually thinking we should get them for Cash, Greg, Jasper, and me, and do an ugly band photo for Insta."

Locke's face lights up. "In that case." He throws the first four he sees into a cart, and I laugh.

"But for real, I have no idea what to get Thorne. What's something that says I'm serious about him?"

"Well, Cash showed me with this." He holds up his left hand where his engagement band sits.

"Yeah, Thorne and I have been together for twenty-four hours. I'm gonna go ahead and say that's *too* serious."

Locke laughs. "Cufflinks? He wears suits a lot."

"That's probably more romantic than Tylenol which is what I have been thinking."

Locke's forehead scrunches in confusion.

"Because the band always gives him a headache."

He laughs. "Hey, that's a good gag gift, but I agree, it doesn't tell him how you feel."

"There's a jewelry store up here. Let's look at the cufflink thing."

The limited assortment the jeweler has doesn't really appeal to me. They all feel impersonal and … blah.

I deflate. One good thing about being in rural Montana is no one has recognized me at all. Not that it's a common occurrence with me anyway—especially not when I'm without Cash, but it lessens the pressure on getting in and out in a hurry. It also probably helps that everyone is distracted trying to fill their own shopping needs.

"I'm back on the Tylenol thing." Just as I say this, a cabinet with men's wedding rings catches my eye. It's true that's so far out of the realm of possibility for now, but next to the rings is something that could work.

Maybe.

When I tell Locke my idea, he immediately tells me to buy it. Then I spend the next hour freaking out that it's too much. Or not enough.

I spin the velvet box in my hand the whole ride back to the house while Locke drives.

When we pull up to the gate, he glances over at me. "It's perfect. I promise. It says everything you need to but without making too big a gesture."

I tuck it into my coat pocket. Christmas is still a few days away, and I don't know if I'll be able to hold on to the gift for that long. I kinda want to throw it at him and run away.

I'm not good at this emotional crap.

Locke laughs at me. "You're freaking out over nothing."

"Not nothing. I don't … I don't know how to do this stuff."

"Give gifts?"

I give him a derisive look. "Smartass."

"Thorne has been into you since as long as I've known him. Anything from you, he'd love, but this …" He points to the bulge in my jacket. "This will make him the happiest man in the world."

That's all I want.

Locke continues. "Other than Cash, I mean. Because let's face it, I'm the best fiancé ever."

I snort. "Of course."

We get out of the car and take the billions of shopping bags out of the back seat.

"How do we sneak these past Cash?" I ask. "He's a nosy fucker, and he's gonna want to see what you got him."

"True." He hands me his bags. "You take them all. I'll distract Cash and Thorne. We'll put them all together."

"I'll drop them off in the room I had with Andrew."

Last night, we stayed in Thorne's room even if there isn't an attached bathroom. It's not that big a deal to stay in there seeing as Andrew's presence in the old room made Thorne uncomfortable.

I make a break for the left and run up the stairs while I see out of the corner of my eye Locke greeting Cash in an over the top display of affection.

"Seb's hiding my presents, isn't he?" Cash asks, and I laugh my way up the steps.

Our plan almost works until I throw open the door to my old room, and Thorne's standing in there unpacking his suitcase.

My eyes widen. "What are you doing in here?"

"You said you didn't have sex in here, right?"

My gaze drops to my pocket even though I tell it not to. *What the hell, eyes? Cooperate, damn it.*

I force myself to focus on Thorne instead. "Right, but, uh, what's wrong with the other room?"

He stares at the billions of bags in my hands. "Are they my presents?"

"And Cash's. Locke's distracting him, and I'm supposed to hide them."

"Oh, in here is fine."

"But I have to hide yours too."

Thorne cocks his head. "It's just sweatpants, right?"

I swallow hard. "Right. Sweatpants. Nothing else."

A smile breaks through on his gorgeous face. "What else is there?"

"Nothing!" Yeah, that sounds believable. I clear my throat. "Uh, nothing, but don't you want the colors to be a surprise?"

"Let me guess. Dark gray, light gray, medium gray, and gray gray."

"Damn it."

"I won't look. I promise." Thorne steps closer. "Also, now that we're together ..." He crooks his finger at me. "I want a kiss hello."

I dump the bags and go willingly.

Our lips meet, his hand cups my face, and then he takes control of my mouth and my body. Then his hands weave into my hair, and I forget my surroundings.

He presses against me, and all I can focus on is his tongue in my mouth, his all-consuming presence, and the way my body immediately wants to melt into him.

His hands release my hair and trail down my back, then skim along my sides, dangerously close to—oh, shit.

I pull away and back out of his grasp.

"What is it?"

"Blowjob!"

Thorne grabs my belt buckle and tugs me toward him. "Mm, yes please. I've wanted my mouth on your cock for so fucking long." He tries to drop to his knees, but I'm too self-conscious about the box in my pocket.

I pull him back up. "No."

"No?"

"I want you to come in my mouth this time."

Thorne moans, and I know I have him. I move him toward the bed and push him down on his back with his legs hanging off the end.

"Take your pants off," I say.

"You're taking control this time?"

"Yep." Because I need to figure out how to blow him while stashing his gift somewhere.

Thorne strips down completely, and I lose my train of thought before I can even move. This man seriously makes me lose brain cells and all thought processing abilities just by taking his clothes off. From his wide chest down to his long, hard cock waiting for my lips.

My mouth waters.

"You going to get naked?" he asks.

"Umm, no." I can't take my jacket off because the box is in there. Then again, maybe I can take it off and throw it into the closet and then chase after it later after Thorne comes his brains out.

"No?" Thorne laughs.

"Uh … I mean, yes." I pull open my coat and slip it off my shoulders, but the minute I throw it, the box drops to the floor a few feet away from me. "Fuck!"

"What? Why are you being weird?"

"I'm not being weird." My voice is definitely being weird though. It's all high-pitched and squeaky. "Ooh, idea." I take off my shirt and throw it to him. "Put that over your eyes."

He takes the shirt cautiously but does it. Damn, that's actually a really hot sight. His long body on display while he can't see anything.

Focus!

I drop to the floor and crawl across the carpet.

"Seb," Thorne rasps. "I need your mouth."

"Working on it." I grab the box and pull it to me, but now what do I do with it? "Maybe you can stroke yourself for me while, I, uh, get my mouth warmed up."

Get my mouth warmed up? What the fuck is wrong with me?

Thorne sits up, my shirt falling from his face. I roll the box under the bed, but I overshoot it, and it disappears into the abyss.

Of course.

"You're definitely being weird," Thorne says.

"Shirt back over your eyes." I blink up at him.

"I feel like you're trying to rob me or something."

"That wouldn't really be worth it, would it? I know how much we pay you."

Thorne laughs, and it seems to settle his unease. He covers his eyes with my shirt again, and no sooner it's back in place, I rise up and lean over him, immediately swallowing his dick to the root.

His hand finds its way into my hair. "Yes. Fuck, yes."

I bring my A game, sucking him deep and stroking the base of his long cock with my hand. This isn't going to last long because I don't want it to.

I glance up at him, at his parted lips and my shirt covering the top half of his face. I wonder how many times he's thought about this moment in the last couple of years. When he's walked in on me with other guys and wished I was hooking up with him instead.

My chest aches that I put him through that. I had no inkling, nothing, about what my actions were doing to him. And now that we're here, his thick cock pulsing in my mouth while I bob my head to draw out his pleasure, I'll do everything it takes to make it up to him.

That's what his gift is about—to let him know I'm all in, and I want this to be a permanent thing.

He groans, low and raspy, and his hips thrust off the bed. I love that even though he's given me control of this situation, and he's trying to restrain himself, he can't manage to do it completely.

I love he desires me that fiercely.

My own cock aches, still stuck behind the confines of my pants because I only managed to get my shirt off in the frantic need to cover up his present. I struggle with my zipper, trying to get my dick free.

My mouth stretches around Thorne's hard length, and I swallow him down. I moan when a dribble of precum hits my tongue because he tastes so fucking good. His cock is perfect. Uncut, long and thick. I can't wait to have it inside me again, but that will have to be another time. I want to taste all of him.

I free my cock and stroke myself just a few times to take away the aching need between my legs long enough to be able to focus everything on Thorne.

"I want to see you," he rasps.

There's no reason he can't now the box is somewhere I can't even see if I'm looking for it, so I reach up and pull my shirt from his eyes. He leans up on his elbows and stares down at me, and the moment our gazes meet, his eyes fill with something I'm not used to seeing from my hookups. There's heat and passion, but I'm struck by the awe and affection there too.

For the first time in my life, my heart feels full. I can't tear my eyes away.

Thorne breaks first. His hand tightens in my hair, his head drops back as his eyes roll and his mouth drops open with the most amazing guttural grunt coming out.

The first spurts of cum shoot down the back of my throat, and I suck harder, swallowing every drop while he keeps convulsing into my mouth. He shudders, his legs tremble, and his muscles uncoil.

I did that. Getting someone off always gives me a power

trip, but with someone I care about? It's so much deeper and intense.

When he finally loosens his hold on my hair and sinks back onto the mattress, his cock falls from my mouth.

He breathes heavily. "I will never get enough of that mouth."

I climb on top of him, straddling his waist and begin to jerk myself off. Thorne doesn't even try to take over, just watches me with a satisfied smile on his face.

He nods. "Come on my chest."

I grunt and do just that. It takes less than a minute of touching myself because I'm so worked up from sucking him dry.

I lean in and fuse my mouth to his, licking into his mouth so he can taste himself on my tongue while strings of cum erupt from my dick and mark his skin.

Thorne kisses me like he'll never get the chance again. That's what's been missing from my life. Every hookup, every groupie, they all knew that it was a one-time deal, yet they didn't kiss me like it was. Or they didn't care it was their only shot. Here I am giving Thorne a promise of more, and he still cherishes my mouth and gives me his all.

Thorne pulls away first, and I complain.

"No."

"No?" He laughs.

"More kissing." I lean in and capture his mouth again, but he only lets me do it for a few seconds.

"I want more, but after dinner. It's our turn to cook, apparently."

I frown. "I have no idea how to cook."

"I'll teach you."

"Orrrr you could do it for me while I sit on the counter and give you moral support with lots of kisses."

Thorne rolls out from underneath me and uses my shirt to wipe my cum off his chest. He stands there naked, looking at me with something like condescending disappointment in his eyes. "You know, one day, you guys aren't going to be the uber famous band you are now, and you're going to have to look after yourselves."

"Nah. I'll still have you."

He pauses and assesses me like he's trying to figure out if I'm being serious or joking. "Hmm, you just said the one thing that could possibly get you out of learning how to cook."

I pull my *I'm so innocent* face. Thorne knows it well.

"You're such a smartass." He throws my shirt back at me and then stalks into the bathroom.

"Is it really being a smartass if it's true?" I call after him.

He grumbles something about emotional manipulation, and I laugh hard.

The fact we can get off with each other but still have the same friendship we've always had afterward is probably the best thing about falling for him.

We're perfect for each other. It might've taken a leaked photo and a stripper to realize that, but I sure as fuck know now.

I just need to convince Thorne I'm for real because I get the distinct impression he still doesn't believe it.

THE LAST FEW days have been an amazing blur of affection and sex with the only person I've ever truly loved with my whole heart.

Seb has eased into the role of partner without any hesitation, but I can't help myself. I'm always looking for a slight flinch at affection or uncomfortableness when the future is mentioned. He hasn't shown any sign of doubt.

Which is weird because I'm full of it. Not so much about us but outside influences. Maybe it's only easy for him because we're hidden away right now. There are no fans, no media, no tabloids.

Here, there's nothing but us, the closest people in the world to us, and ... well, Jasper's groupie, but she's pretty nice. Yesterday on the eve of Christmas Eve, we found a freshly cut Christmas tree and decorations outside the front door.

We spent the afternoon putting it up and then Locke whipped out four ugly Christmas sweaters for the band to wear in front of it to post on Instagram. The notifications have been blowing up my phone ever since, so I've turned it to silent. I would've left it in our bedroom, but I need to be able to check it every now and then to make sure no other crappy scandals have broken out.

A manager's job is never done.

None of us had organized the tree, and my only thought was of Mason. He had to be the one to have done it, and that makes me smile. He can't be as bitter as he led on if he's throwing Christmas spirit on our doorstep.

I'm still hoping he'll make an appearance tomorrow like I told him to, but I'm not holding my breath. We'll see what Christmas brings.

At the moment, all I'm focused on is me and Seb. We're outside by the fire again, a spot that's quickly becoming our favorite.

We're under a blanket on a long deck chair, and he's resting his back against my front. The lounger is narrow so my feet hang off the sides and it's not the most comfortable, but when Seb's in my arms, I'm too warm and settled to move.

Everyone else has long gone to bed, but I could stay out here forever. Or until the fire dies out and we start freezing to death—literally.

I kiss the top of his head. "Christmas tomorrow."

"Mmhmm," he says sleepily.

"Maybe we should go to bed so Santa can come."

"Is that my nickname now? You want to go upstairs so *Santa* can come?"

"Only you can turn the sanctity of Christmas into something dirty."

"It's a gift, but for real, if you want to go to bed and fuck me, I'll take one for the team. It will be soooo hard."

"It's late, and you're tired rambling. What if we went to bed and fell asleep instead?"

"Fine. Christmas morning blowjob then."

I huff. "Sure, baby. Whatever you want."

He turns his head to look up at me. "What do *you* want?"

"Honestly, this." I tighten my arms around him. "Don't get me wrong, the sex is amazing, and I want more, but I enjoy holding you just as much."

His lips brush against mine, and his beard tickles my skin.

"I've never had that before," he admits softly.

"I can give you more than sex. You're worth more than that, Seb."

Seb's dark eyes close, and he nuzzles into my neck. I pretend I don't feel the wetness on my skin because he won't appreciate me calling him out for crying even if it's to point out his feelings are perfectly valid and I'm sorry for every asshole who has used him in his life.

"Let's go to bed," I whisper, and he nods against me.

We stumble upstairs and strip each other down. I kiss his skin and run my hands all over him, and even though I'm hard as hell and love Seb's naked body, I'd rather feed him reassurance than my cock.

We lie in each other's arms, and I don't plan to let him go all night. He falls asleep fast, his breathing evening out, but like I have for the last few nights, I stay awake, basking in the surrealness of having Seb by my side.

He murmurs something in his sleep, but I can't make it out.

"What was that?"

"Love you," he mumbles.

My heart explodes all over again. We haven't used the L word again since we first admitted our feelings for each other. Honestly, I've been scared to.

There's a difference between admitting I'm in love with him in an abstract concept and saying those three little words that mean the world. Even though I'm ninety-five percent sure he's asleep and isn't aware of what he's saying, I kiss the top of his head and say, "I love you too."

$$\oint$$

I don't think I've been this excited to wake up on Christmas since I was a kid. I'm looking forward to my wake-up blowjob, but that falls apart when Cash runs through the house like the child he is, screaming, "It's Christmas, bitches!"

Hmm, a child who swears a lot.

"I guess that means we're being summoned to the tree," I say.

Seb groans. "Mm, five more minutes, Mom."

"Come on. I'm eager to open my brand new watches you guys always seem to get me every year."

Seb smiles but doesn't open his eyes. "We really should've learned to coordinate by now."

It's kind of become a running joke. The first time it happened, our first Christmas together, the band had just hit it big and they had money to burn. I got four Rolexes. Now they do it just to fuck with me, and each year, it's as if they try to outdo each other in getting me the most gaudy and expensive, diamond encrusted thing they can find. Each year there's a winner for ugliest watch.

It's ridiculous, but I still own all of them even though I never wear them.

We get up and put on sweats. On my way out of the room, Seb says he'll meet me downstairs.

I find Locke in the kitchen getting coffee for everyone while the rest of the band is sitting on the floor near the tree. Cash is even wearing a Santa hat he pulled from God knows where.

None of us are with our blood relatives this year, but there's no other place I'd rather be than with our band family.

I sit with the guys, and Seb comes down not long later and takes his spot next to me.

"Where's your groupie?" I ask Jasper.

"I told her to sleep in considering I don't have a present for her. It would be awkward for her to sit here while we're all giving each other gifts."

I shake my head at him. "You didn't think to go *buy* her something?"

"Oh. Right. That probably would've been a good idea," Jasper says.

I laugh. "You're all clueless."

"Hey, I'm not." Cash jumps up to reach for the first present and hands it to Locke.

"Wow. I guess fiancé beats best friend," Seb says dryly.

"Yep." Cash has no remorse whatsoever.

"I can fix that." I lean forward to get the present I put together for Seb.

Just like the guys have done with my watches, I've made the habit of collecting guitar picks for Seb. He goes through them like crazy—flinging them into the crowd for fans at every show—and even though they're a business expense and not exactly romantic, I always try to find unique designs.

He's expecting them, but his face lights up anyway. Unlike every other time I've given him a new set of picks, he leans in and thanks me with a kiss.

"Yeah, that's still going to take a while to get used to," Cash says.

Seb pulls away and flips him off.

We all exchange gifts, I get about ten pairs of sweatpants from Seb which confuses the rest of the band, but we don't elaborate on our inside joke. The pile of gifts dwindles away until there're only four identical boxes left.

All four bandmembers stare at me while I unwrap each individual one and choose the ugliest. They don't label who they're from anymore, and they all use the same wrapping paper so I can't tell who bought what.

The first one I open is a contender for sure. Gold skulls and snakes wrap around the face of the watch.

"Wow. Umm, thank you so much."

Everyone snickers.

The next doesn't even look like a watch at all. It looks more like the inside of a machine. It must be expensive. It's ugly as fuck and doesn't make any sense.

Then there's a Hysek which probably costs more than my car, hell probably more than my house, but while it's ugly, it's not gaudy.

The last one though. Holy shit that takes the cake. "We have a winner." I hold up the gold-plated watch that has different stones in the shape of Kanye West on the face.

Seb nudges me. "I know how you feel about Kanye and knew how much you'd *hate* it."

"You did this?"

He smiles smugly. "Booyah. I win this year."

The other three grumble, but I'm oddly touched that he'd know this would win because of my strong aversion to the most egotistical artist in the industry. That's not even defamation, it's just fact.

"Who wants breakfast?" Locke stands.

I get up too. "I'll help."

Something passes between Locke and Seb, and Locke waves me off. "No, no. I can do it. Or better yet, Cash, get your ass up."

"I have to cook again?" Cash complains but stands anyway.

"Yes." Locke nudges him and then nods in our direction, and I have no idea what that's supposed to mean.

Seb grabs my hand. "Come with me. I have one more present for you."

"You do?"

"Yep. And do you know how hard it was to hide while blowing you?"

I burst out laughing. "That's what that was?"

"Yep."

That's actually ... kind of a relief. I thought he was acting weird because of doubt, but when it didn't happen again, I chalked it up to a passing moment. Knowing he was trying to hide a present for me gives me some reassurance in this very new relationship.

Seb leads me to the front closet where our thick jackets are.

"We're going somewhere?"

"Just out back to the firepit. I kinda don't want an audience for this."

"For what?"

"You can just wait. I've been keeping this under wraps for days. I'm not going to ruin it now." He leads me outside, holding my hand the whole way. The fire isn't lit, and when I go to the firewood to build it, Seb pulls me back. "We won't be out here long."

We press against each other, and I bask in his warmth.

Seb swallows hard and takes a deep breath.

"Why are you nervous?" I ask.

"This is ... kinda big." His eyes widen. "Oh God, not like the biggest thing I'm ever going to give you ever ... now it sounds like I'm talking about my dick. I'm not. Oh shit, I'm fucking this up. Okay, let's pretend none of that fell from my mouth. Redo! Umm ..."

I lean in and kiss his bearded cheek. "Whatever it is, I'll love it. You don't need to feel any pressure, okay?"

He shakes it off and tries again. "I wanted to get you something that shows you I'm taking us seriously. That I'm all in."

"I'm all in too," I murmur. "Is that the present? A promise?"

Seb clears his throat. "It's a little more than that. Umm. So ..."

"Are you sweating?" I have to admit it's kind of cute.

"When I asked Locke what kind of gift screams serious, he flashed his engagement ring."

My breath gets caught in my throat because yes, I may know this man is the love of my life, but marriage is ... like— My thoughts are cut off by Seb's laughter.

"Your face was my reaction too. No way are we *there* yet. But ... I got you this." He pulls out a small ring box and squeezes it in his hand. "It's not an engagement ring, so you can breathe."

Oh. Right. Kinda need to do that.

"Maybe you should just open it." Seb flattens his palm, offering me the box.

My heart beats fast even though he just told me it's not a ring, but when I open it slowly, I'm confused. Because it *is* a ring.

Seb pulls it out of the slot, and following it comes a long chain. "I wanted you to know that our future is right here. I'm optimistic that I've found my forever person, and while it's way too early for that, it's not early to tell you that I plan for it to happen. One day."

"Holy shit." My words come out with puffs of steam.

My nose is frozen, my eyes are watery, and if we don't get out of this cold soon, we'll freeze, but I don't care.

He pulls the chain open, and I duck my head so he can put it around my neck. "Until that day comes, I want you to wear this so you'll always know how much I want to be with you and make this work."

With this one gesture, any remaining doubt or hesitance about doing this is completely gone.

"It won't be easy. I'm going to mess up and piss you off, but I know with my whole heart that you're my future, Thorne. You're everything I've wanted wrapped in a package I thought I could never have."

"I'm yours, Seb."

His warm eyes meet mine. "I love you."

With his ring sitting next to my heart, I'm going to be reminded every day that his words are true.

"I love you too."

When Seb kisses me, he runs his hand over the chain hanging around my neck.

A symbol of our future.

A promise to try.

He breaks the kiss and presses his forehead against mine. "One day, when we're both ready, you'll give me this ring and tell me it's time."

I let out a small laugh. "Why's that my responsibility?"

"Because you're the responsible one in this relationship. Duh."

That is true. "Okay. Deal."

"Now we should get inside before you freeze all your good parts off and you can't use them later."

"Wouldn't want that," I snark.

"Hell no."

When we go back inside, the rest of the band scramble away from the windows as if they weren't just watching that play out, but they've added someone to the mix.

"Mason?" I say.

Mason Nash runs his hand over the back of his hair. "That offer for Christmas still good? My family did Christmas last night and all went to my brother-in-law's. I thought I might come hang out up here. I, uh, brought leftover food. Mom always makes too much."

I approach him and throw my arms around him. "You're always welcome … at your own house."

He laughs. "Thanks."

"Merry Christmas."

"You too."

"I'm happy you came."

When I get back to Seb, all he does is lean in and mutter, "That's Mason Nash? What happened?"

I shake my head. "I have no idea. He's tight-lipped about it all."

"He looks …"

Mason's gaze flicks to us.

"Hot," I say for him.

"I was going to say different. You really have a thing for guys with beards, huh?"

"Ooh, yeah. Could you also see if you can borrow some flannel from him? I have a lumberjack fantasy I want to play out."

"Only if I get to play with an ax."

I really have to think about that. "Maybe I'll keep that a fantasy. I don't entirely trust you with sharp things."

He points at me. "And that's why you're the responsible

one." He kisses me quickly and then runs off to tackle Cash on the couch. Because that's just who they are.

We spend the day drinking and eating and literally being the textbook definition of merry. Even Mason seems to have fun.

This might possibly go down in history as the best band vacation ever.

I CAN'T TAKE my eyes off Seb as he kicks ass onstage. He's shirtless, his long hair falling past his shoulders and covering his face as he rocks out to the band's greatest hits. Like he always does, he puts everything into his performance. It's impossible to look at anything else other than him because he's so damn charismatic. And he's all mine.

It's only been two months since we left Montana for the Southern Hemisphere—first the Asia circuit, then New Zealand, and now we're down under. From the freezing cold to Australia's harsh summer, the contrast fits with the shift in Seb's and my relationship.

My fingers fiddle with the ring around my neck through my shirt. Honestly, it took about a week until the itch to take it off and slip it on my finger kicked in.

And Seb thought he'd be the one to jump the gun.

I keep reminding myself it's too soon. In some ways we're still really new. In other ways, it feels like we've been together since the beginning.

The worry over fans wanting him has been far from my

mind as he has no shame pointing me out during meet and greets. Even though I told him he doesn't have to out us if he didn't want—that from a manager's standpoint, appearing single is always better so the mania surrounding the band's lives is hyped up—he has never once hesitated to say he's taken.

The story of us has leaked into the media a little, but I'm sure once we're back stateside, it will explode even more. We've already heard from the label about their disapproval and have had talks about getting the band a new manager, but Cash stepped in and basically told the execs he'd walk if they so much as touched me. Cash Me Outside without Cash Kingsley would be like Bon Jovi without Jon. It just wouldn't work.

With the band's full support, Seb and I know that whatever happens, we're ready for it. I think we're ready for a lot. He has shown me in the last two months that he can handle the job while being in a relationship with me.

I fidget with the ring again.

It's too soon, Thorne. Way too soon.

The show is getting toward the end, so Cash ducks offstage for one last wardrobe change before the final song and then encore. While he's gone, Seb entertains the crowd.

"It's hot as balls out here tonight!"

That's my man.

The crowd screams and eats up his onstage persona like they always do. They don't get to see the man I know deep down. The one who comes home with me after a show and lets down his walls.

The one who begs me to fuck him and then murmurs how much he loves me before we fall asleep.

When Cash goes back onstage for the last song, the pyro starts up.

Maybe if I was paying attention to the wider surroundings and not so stuck on Seb, I would see it sooner—the firework aimed right at him.

Dread sinks like lead when it goes off, and I see what's happening.

I fucking told Cash the pyro was too much. I *told* him.

And now, as everything happens in slow motion yet too fast, my heart jumps into my throat because I know I can't get to Seb in time.

The firework shoots into the air, on a mission to take off Seb's head. My feet scramble to work. To run to him. But I won't make it.

"Seb!" I call out, but like my vision, it's too slow. Too soft. It comes out in a panicked gasp.

I'm not fast enough, and the fear that slices through my gut is crippling.

In this moment, I fear the worst, and instead of thinking about saving him, all I can think about is regret. I regret holding out. I regret not having his ring on my finger.

Why the fuck did we wait?

By some miracle, Seb sees it and has fast enough reflexes to throw his entire body flat onto the stage, his guitar landing under him with a loud crash.

The firework shoots over the top of him, clipping a stage light above him and sending it falling just a few feet from his flattened body.

Chaos rings out, the sound of shattered glass echoes in my ear, but I'm still not moving.

Why can't I move?

The crowd screams in horror, but it's all background noise.

Finally, my feet unlock from their spot, and I rush onstage, not giving a shit seventeen thousand pairs of eyes are on me. It's my job to be invisible, but I can't be this time. Not with this.

Not with *him*.

I hook my arms under Seb and lift him to drag him offstage so I can assess any damage. His broken guitar is still strapped to him, so I take that off and then hold him close.

He's wide-eyed and silent, probably in shock.

"I've got you," I murmur.

He trembles in my arms, his clammy skin breaking out in goose bumps.

I lead him to sit on an amp box and take my suit jacket off to wrap around him. It's hot as sin out here, but he's shivering. Getting on my knees, I run my hands over him to check him over.

Backstage crew swarm us, but I shoo them all away. "I've got this. Give him some space." I turn to Seb. "Are you hurt?"

Seb swats at my hands. "I'm fine. Stop fussing."

I'd believe that more if he wasn't shaking.

"Seb—"

He seems to shake out of whatever shocked trance he's in. "I'm fine. I promise. I just ... Fuck, that was crazy."

"Whoever set up the pyro is fucking fired," I grit out.

Seb takes a deep breath and smiles. "No. They're not."

"What?" I shriek.

"You know what I saw right before I thought I was dead?"

Cash and Greg appear at our sides.

"What was that?" Cash asks and turns to me. "What do we do? There's broken glass all over the stage."

Right. Shit. I need to be in manager mode right now.

"Show's over. You were on the last song, and no one will blame you guys for cutting it short."

"No, we should finish the set," Seb says and tries to stand.

"Are you kidding me?" I push him back down. "You're not going back out there."

"We can't end a show like that." He points to the stage where crew members are already clearing away the debris.

"No, but I can end a show with this." Cash grabs his nearby guitar. "If you're not up for it. We should do *something* else."

I nod. "Cash, you go out there. Finish with an acoustic song you can sing by yourself. The others can go back to the dressing room and get ready to leave to go to the hotel. I wouldn't mind taking Seb to the hospital to have him checked out."

"What? I don't need a hospital."

I glare at him. "Yes, you do. I thought I was going to lose you." My voice cracks, but I can't help it.

Seb shakes his head. "Never."

My nose tingles, and my eyes hurt because I almost lost him. One tiny mistake by the crew, and I could've lost him forever.

Now more than ever, I know I don't want to have this ring around my neck. It belongs on my finger, Seb belongs at my side, and as if reading my very thoughts, Seb leans forward and cups my face with his callused hands.

"Some people say that your life flashes before your eyes before you die, but all I could see was your face. *You.* It's not the band or fame or groupies, it's you." He runs his finger under the chain around my neck and untucks it from my shirt. "I've been trying to be patient, Thorne, but every day you make it harder and harder to remind myself it's too soon."

My hand covers his. "Me too," I admit.

"And after that?" His brown eyes pierce through me, cutting into my soul. "Why are we waiting?"

The answer to that is I really don't know.

So here I am, already on my knees before him, with a ring in his hand. So I blurt out what I've been holding in ever since we got to Australia.

"Marry me?"

"Fuck yes. It's about damn time."

"We've been dating for two months," I point out. "By society's standards, this is fast."

"It's been so much longer than two months. I just didn't know it. I love you with everything that I am, and I think I have for a long time." Seb's lips brush against mine. "Besides, by celebrity standards, this is slow."

"Well, you are a celebrity."

"I'd give it up in a heartbeat if you asked me to."

"I would never do that. You are this life." And it's one of the reasons I love him. The fact he wanted to give his fans more even though he could've been seriously injured just now … it speaks to my inner workaholic, and I find it an extremely attractive trait for him to have.

"You're more important," Seb says. "I honestly didn't know how I was going to be a good boyfriend or if I was even relationship material, but with you, I haven't even had to think about it. I want you there by my side when I go to sleep and when I wake up. I want you to be the one to drag me out of bed when I have media to face or songs to write. I want to be yours."

"Be mine. Forever."

Seb smiles his trademark smirk. "I wouldn't settle for anything less."

THANK YOU

Oh, Sebastian and your demanding fans. You couldn't just leave well enough alone, could you? You had to have your time in the spotlight. You're the reason poor Mason was still hiding in Montana long after he was supposed to already have his book! But Mason's story is here now.
Fandom, Famous Book Three is available here:
https://geni.us/jDflqR

Want to read about Mason's ex-bandmates? Harley Valentine is trying desperately to get the band back together. Read his story here in *Pop Star, Famous Book One*:
https://geni.us/faAAP

Also out now: *Spotlight, Famous Book Two*. Cash makes his first appearance here! https://geni.us/XImSg

Want to stay up to date on everything Eden Finley?
Join my reader group here:
https://www.facebook.com/groups/absolutelyeden/

https://amzn.to/2zUlM16

https://www.edenfinley.com

FAMOUS SERIES

Pop Star

Spotlight

Fandom

Novellas:

Locked Heart

Thorned Heart

FAKE BOYFRIEND SERIES

Fake Out

Trick Play

Deke

Blindsided

Hat Trick

Novellas:

Fake Boyfriend Breakaways: A short story collection

Final Play

STEELE BROTHERS

Unwritten Law

Unspoken Vow

BOOKS COWRITTEN WITH SAXON JAMES

Power Plays & Straight A's

Face Offs & Cheap Shots

Goal Lines & First Times

Line Mates & Study Dates

STANDALONES

Headstrong

(Part of Sarina Bowen's World of True North)

ACKNOWLEDGMENTS

I want to thank my long list of betas, especially Leslie
Copeland from Les Court Services. Sandra from One Love
editing for copy-edits.
Thanks to Lori Parks for one last read through for those ninja
typos that have the ability to sneak through four rounds of
editing.
And lastly, thanks to Cate Ashwood for designing the cover.

Made in the USA
Monee, IL
15 May 2021